# The Trial of Trump's Assassin

*R. G. Coleman, Ph.D.*

# Books by R.G. Coleman, Ph.D.

*The People v George "Dubya"Bush*

*The Governor's Fingerprints*

*A Mom's Perfect Murder?*

*God: for Smart and Funny People Only*

*Justice for Baby Josh*

*Good Dad – Bad Mom – The Criminalization of a
Father's Paternal Instincts – Part One*

*Good Dad – Bad Mom – The Criminalization of a
Father's Paternal Instincts – Part Two*

*Johnny Carson, Ted Williams, and Me*

*Trump's Troops Revolt Against Republican
Party's Betrayal*

*Why and How We, The People, Must
RemoveTrump*

*The "Gang of Seven Judges" & Crimes They
Committed*

## R. G. Coleman as Jocelyn Dr. Otis Coleman
*My One-Night Stand With God's Assassin*

*My Daughter's Keeper*

## The United States District Court
## For the District of Columbia

## Day One

Judge Jessie Vance: "In the case of the Government of the United States versus Dr. Richard Otis, are the parties ready to proceed?"

"Federal Prosecutor Meyer Brody for the Government your Honor. We are ready to proceed."

"Dr. Richard Otis, Defendant, *pro se,* Judge."

Handing copies to the Bailiff and Brody, Dr. Otis continues, "The Defendant herein offers his revised objections to the Court's denial of his Pretrial motion pursuant to 28 US. Code #455(a) --"

Brody; "Objection Your Honor, FRCP, Local Rule 49, prohibits litigants from directing motions, pleadings, and correspondence directly to the Judge,"

Judge Vance: Where is your counselor?"

"I choose to represent myself."

"You understand you are being charged under 18 U.S. Code #1751 (a)(i) -- "Whoever kills an individual who is President of the United States ...shall be punished by Section 1111 of this title," to wit, "the unlawful killing with malice aforethought is murder in the First Degree, punishable by death, unless the jury qualifies its verdict  by adding without capital punishment for  imprisonment for life."

Dr. Otis: "The State falsely characterizes my action as unlawful killing with malice aforethought, when the State knows, or should know, that rather than malice  aforethought, I acted out of labored conscience, devotion,  and duty to protect America against a consensus enemy.'

Brody: "Objection, Your Honor. The Defendant has strayed from his Motion objecting to the Pretrial dismissal of his motions to a rambling diatribe sounding like a misplaced opening statement!"

Judge Vance: Though you are *pro se*, Mr.-

Dr. Otis, "Otis, Judge, Dr. Otis."

Judge Vance: – "Dr. Otis, You can expect no special treatment from this Court. That said,  you should rethink your decision to represent yourself given the fact that your conviction for assassinating the President of the United States will result in a death sentence."

Dr. Otis: "I appreciate your words of caution, but I don't share your dire prediction. I appear on my own behalf believing that the jury will see that which the Government defines as "assassination," as instead protecting Americans from a President who, by seizing control of America's courts –  particularly the United States Supreme Court, Congress, the US Senate, the Executive, judicial, and Legislative Branches of Government, the Republican Party, the media – his hands being around the throat of FOX News, which is not news – makes no attempt to be news, but rather is a blatant Conservative propaganda conduit to control the hearts and minds of Americans – a fraud founded by Reagan's planted Conservative FCC members -- Trump's control of the military, the economy, business, commerce, trade, tariff's, treaties, our relations with other countries and the lives of immigrants seeking asylum in the United States, rump has so bullied and slandered any and all who opposed him –thus turning America into a house divided, not witnessed since the Civil War, all under the thumb of a dictator.

Trump has imposed his personal *Weltanschauung* on Americans by his hourly blitzkrieg of narcissistic tweets, has manipulated Trump's "troops" – Neo-Nazi/white supremacists, like Hitler's brown shirts, poised to *de facto*overthrow the Constitutional Republic at Trump's whim.

Trump, America's President turned Dictator, anointed himself king – becoming Rome's Emperor Caligula, so proselytizing Americans and so vitiating their Constitution, as to represent a clear and present danger to the Republic and its citizens, left no other remedy to save the Republic from Trump's tyranny!"

Brody: "Your Honor, the Defendant has turned his reasons for *pro se* representation into an opening statement!"

Judge Vance: "I was about to say the same. Move on. Mr. --"

Dr. Otis: "Otis, judge. Otis. The point being that my decision to represent myself acknowledges the maxim, "He who represents himself has a fool for a client," while yielding to a more omniscient bromide, "Truth is the ultimate arbiter in all matters.""

Judge Vance: "The American system of criminal justice is adversarial depending on contesting arguments presented by skilled attorneys representing the prosecution and the defense in a legal process resulting in a fair and just ruling."

Dr. Otis: "Or, as my wives two and four, stated, "The best lie wins."(It did for # two, but not for four.)

Judge Vance: "Have you had any prior legal training or experience?"

Dr. Otis: "Unable to afford attorney's retainersfor more than I would recover, unable to pay a lawyer $300 an hour, yet unwilling to accept injustice, fraud, deceptive business practices, corrupt cops, and "dirty judges," -- yes, a black robe does not a honest judge make, any more than a black priest's robe makes a "pure" prelate – I have represented myself *pro se* in a number of cases –"

Brody: "Seventeen and counting"_

Dr. Otis: "-- won a few – child molestation against one of my son's coaches --an appeal against a superior court judge – court's are the people's business, but judge's talk about, "my courtroom," lawyer's see courts as their 'store" and Clerk's of Court are instructed to tell the public, "Get a lawyer," as if the public is an intruder, trespasser, and/or presumed guilty"

Brody: "Your Honor, the Defendant, suddenly realizing a death sentence is in his future, relives his brief encounter playing Clarence Darrow as a stalling tactic."

Judge Vance: "Having established that you have waived your right to appointed counsel despite my efforts to dissuade you otherwise, I concur with the Prosecutor."

Dr. Otis: "I apologize for having unwittingly strayed from the course of my intended focus, to wit, my Pretrial motions for your recusal, jurisdiction issues, change of venue, and the Government's violations of my14[th] Amendment guarantees of a fair and impartial adjudication of my defenses as well as my equal protection under the laws."

Brody: "More delaying tactics, Your Honor."

Judge Vance: "The Court is in no rush to judgment in a capital murder case, particularly when the Defendant is *pro se*. That said, The Prosecutor's position must not be ignored."

Dr. Otis: "Fair enough. Attorneys generally perceived by the public, and therefore jurors, to be liars for hire to the highest – richest – bidder, would seem to be a liability to me, whose case depends on this simple truth: Trump's coup d'état – his overthrow of the government United States of America had become a *fait accompli* with his Hitleresque -- Putinesque control of the government, the military, the media and therefore the American people leaving only two alternatives to save the Republic – Revolution – five years too soon – I prefer an honest death to a dishonest "Not Guilty" verdict."

Brody: "Your Honor!"Now  the Defendant his making his  closing argument!"

Dr. Otis: "-- As to my 14th Amendment guarantees of equal protection under the laws, I argue as follows; First, the Judge and Prosecutor being both employees of the same Government which is the named plaintiff/adversary in this case, gives unfair advantage to the Government, in turn, inviting the charge that my

14th Amendment right to "equal protection under the laws," is already compromised before the trial begins.

Second, the Constitution of the United States guarantees every citizen a "fair and impartial judiciary," begging the questions: (1) Given the fact that Judges are drawn from the ruling class, for example, all the current US Supreme Court Judges are  Harvard or Yale Law School graduates except Justice Ginsburg who transferred to Columbia, how likely is it that I, an indigent, *pro se* litigant, will  receive a "fair and impartial judicial consideration of my case? Very unlikely. On appeal to the Conservative biased US Supreme Court on its merits? Never!

Third, even allowing for a court-appointed attorney, what are the odds of me receiving the same quality of representation as I would receive if I were a Harvard  or Yale "legacy," a  billionaire's progeny, or Fred Trump's son? Zero.

Fourth and foremost, by seating as many Supreme Court Judges in his first 28 months as Clinton, Bush II, and Obama each did in 8 years, Trump completed the unconstitutional and criminal Conservative coup of the United States Supreme Court … I noted that you are a Bush II appointment, and therefore, by definition, a Conservative Judge, predetermined to rule against my liberal/progressive cause regardless of the merits of my case, and most certainly to rule against me for having disrupted extremist  Conservative president Trump's Conservative overthrow of the Federal judiciary… 28 US. Code #455(a) states, "Any judge or magistrate judge of the United States shall disqualify himself in any proceeding in which his impartiality mightreasonably be questioned." Any circumstance in which a judge's impartiality might reasonably be questioned under § 455 (a) requires disqualification, even if the circumstance is not enumerated as in § 455(b)," *Liljeberg v. Health Servs. Acquisition Corp.*

When the impartiality of a judge is in doubt, the appropriate remedy is to disqualify that judge from hearing further proceedings in the matter."

Therefore, I herein move that you disqualify yourself based on the fact that having been appointed by Conservative ex-President George "Dubya" Bush, you too must be Conservative, otherwise Bush would not have nominated you, thereby denying me due process right to an impartial adjudication in this case – exposing me to an "outward manifestation of what could reasonably be construed as bias" leading to consequences so dire – a death sentence – that disqualification is required, *United States v. Bobo."*

Judge Vance. "My having been appointed by President Bush is not sufficient grounds for disqualification."

Dr. Otis: "Any circumstance in which a judge's impartiality might reasonably be questioned under § 455 (a) requires disqualification, The circumstances in this case in which your impartiality  might be questioned include, but are not limited to: (1) Having been appointed by Conservative President Bush, as a card carrying Conservative espousing Conservative dogma and practices disqualifies you from presiding as a "fair and impartial judge as  guaranteed me by the 14th Amendment of Constitution of the United States. Therefore your impartiality is reasonably questioned and you must disqualify yourself as a matter of law.  (2)

You cannot simultaneously represent yourself to the public as a Conservative Judge and a fair and impartial judge – they are mutually exclusive representations, just as you could not assert that you are a Catholic and an atheist.

Therefore your impartiality is reasonably questioned and you must disqualify yourself as a matter of law. (3) As a devout Conservative awarded your judgeship by then Conservative President of the United States, Bush, your impartiality in a case before this Court, in which the Defendant is charged with assassinating another Conservative president, must be reasonably questioned . Therefore, you must disqualify yourself from the case at bar pursuant to 28 US. Code #455(a).

(4) The fact that the Government is prosecuting me for allegedly assassinating the leader of the extremist right-wing of the Neo-Conservative Republican Party succeeds as to 28 US Code #455, where other reasons may equivocate.

Furthermore, your fraudulent refusal  to disqualify yourself should vitiate all your subsequent Orders, rulings, and findings in this case."

Judge Vance; "Are you threatening me?"

Dr. Otis: "Merely citing Code #455(a), Judge".

Judge Vance: "I need not be so advised by a *pro se* litigant as to what the law says."

Dr. Otis: "That statement confirms bias against me of a different, but no less virulent kind, which, when added to the above noted other prejudices, supports my contention that a neutral court must be sought -- the International Criminal Court in the Hague comes to mind."

Judge Vance: "Sorry, the United States is not a member of the ICC."

Dr. Otis: "Your point is well taken. I forgot that in 1998, the vote to join the International Criminal Court  was 120 countries voting for membership and only seven against –Iraq, Israel, Libya, China Qatar, Yemen, and the United States – conservative extremist countries every one."

Judge Vance: "Well, there you have it: The United States is not a party to the Rome Statute establishing the ICC. No ICC membership, no jurisdiction."

Dr. Otis; "Not so fast. In 2000 President Clinton, signed to join the ICC, but couldn't get the Conservative Senate to ratify the treaty. On May 6th, 2002, the same President Bush II who appointed you, undid Clinton's bid to join the ICC by writing to the Secretary General of the United Nations that the United States had no intention to join the other 123 ICC member countries. I would also parenthetically remind you that your own Conservative Republican Bush also jumped ship  to become the only country NOT signing the Kyoto Accords, pulled out of the International Planned Parenthood Federation, the Anti-Ballistic Missile Treaty, the 156 nations supporting the ban on land mines, the Convention on the Elimination of all forms of Discrimination against Women, the Convention on the rights of the Child, the Convention against the deployment of Biological Weapons, START II – Russia and US agreed to limit the range of their respective nuclear weapons, the International Convention on the Elimination of all forms of Discrimination, and the Geneva Conventions – Article

3 – the prohibition against torture of prisoners. Your Bush II – always a highwayman along the "low road,"in a bad faith effort to avoid Article 3, just as he had avoided active duty in the Vietnam War by deserting his Texas Air National Guard unit, violated the substance and intent of Article 3, by renaming his prisoners "enemy combatants," illegally imprisoning them outside American soil at Guantanamo in Cuba, without probable cause, without telling them of the charges against them, denying them a trial, and then thumbing his nose at Article 26 of the Geneva Convention, which states in pertinent part, that every country ratifying the Geneva Conventions, (including the United States), is bound to perform and conform to Geneva Convention provisions "in good faith." (Bush's torture, of "enemy combatants," denying them their rights and protections of the Geneva Conventions, denying that al Qaeda and Taliban prisoners are entitled to Geneva Conventions protections, and "Dubya's" "Military Preemption Doctrine,' were all clear and compelling evidence that your sponsor, Conservative President Bush  committed multiple violations of the Geneva Conventions and International Law sufficient to invite the charges of "international outlaw," -- committing war crimes and crimes against humanity – without forgetting his most heinous war crimes – his illicit invasion of Afghanistan and his fraudulently declared war on Iraq – "Dubya's" self-indulgent vanities on display in this brief  linking Bush II to a diagnosis of Narcissistic Personality Disorder.

Bush II's reign of errors, whose every act was to reinforce Dubya's delusion of being Number One in the World, to soon be replicated by Narcissistic Personality

Disorder Trump,  whose every act was to prove
Donald's delusion that he is Number One in the World.
Meanwhile, Bush II, sent some 10,000 American
soldiers to die in Afghanistan and Iraq – to prove to
Mommy Bush that "Little Georgie" was favored over
all others, including Poppy Bush, who chose not to
invade Iraq during Desert Storm and not to "take out"
Saddam Hussein, thereby opening the door of
opportunity to his opportunist son,"Dubya" to finally
outdo and out-duel Bush I. (Recall Poppy Bush was an
All-Star first baseman at Yale, while Dubya was an all-
fraternity drunk. Poppy was a World War II hero and
medal winning pilot. Dubya deserted his Texas Air
National Guard unit to avoid being sent to active duty
in Vietnam.Poppy made his fortune in Texas oil. Dubya
sold his Arbusto Oil Company to Harvard-based bailout investors on illegal  insider stock information before
it tanked. Poppy was a much loved, loyal, and honest
president, while Dubya was a sleazy con-man who lied
to Congress, lied to the UN and lied to the American
people that Saddam had  biological and chemical
weapons and weapons of mass destruction, none of
which were ever found."

Brody: "Irrelevance, Your Honor; President
Bush is not a party to this present case, therefore I move
that the entire statements made by the Defendant be
stricken."

Dr. Otis: "To the contrary, Conservative Bush
II, having appointed you to your judgeship, due to your
Conservative biases is very much a not-so- silent party
to these matters in general, and specifically as to my
thesis that you, as an appointee of Conservative
Republican Bush II, cannot, and will not, administer a

fair and impartial hearing and ruling in this matter, thereby making the case for a change of venue to an international tribunal in which the Government of the United States is not a *de facto* interested party, to wit the named Plaintiff!.

Furthermore, the fact that Ultra-Conservative Donald Trump entrenched himself as the State - "L'etatc'estmoi," compels us to seek jurisdiction of a neutral court in which the Government of the United States is not a *de facto* interested party.

That argument draws support from the similarities between Bush II and Trump I, who  like Little Bush, is also a Narcissistic Personality Disorder, and who, like Bush's presidency, is an outward manifestation of his pathological narcissism,

For example, both  "Georgie" and "Donnie" suffered from the primary symptom of a Narcissistic Personality Disorder, to wit, both suffered from debilitating, dangerous, and regime-threatening delusions of grandeur that each, in turn, believed he was Number One in the world, *uber alles,* and each governed, not the people, but to confirm their delusion of greatness unsupported by reality.

So for example, the first order of governance for both Bush II and Trump I-- hopefully there will never be a Trump II, was to  assert superiority over their predecessor, Bush trashed all things Clinton, Trump trumped all things Obama, Dubya skipped out on Clinton's Kyoto Accords, Trump skipped out on Obama's Paris Agreement, Dubya thumbed his nose at the International Planned Parenthood Federation. Trump castrated Planned Parenthood by cutting its funds, Bush reneged  on Clinton's  Anti-Ballistic

Missile Treaty, and the 156 nations supporting the ban on land mines. Trump pulled out of the Intermediate Range Nuclear Forces Treaty. Democrat Clinton inherited a $290 billion deficit from Republican Reagan and Bush I's "trickle-down economics," which Clinton turned into surpluses each of the last three years of his presidency. Trump bequeathed Biden a four Trillion dollar deficit caused by Trump's political self-interest refusal to timely limit the deadly invasion of the COVID -19 pandemic. Republican Bush II, reinstated "trickle-down/de-regulation economics" causing the third Republican Depression – Hoover, Reagan, and Bush II, with Dubya's Depression being the direct cause  of millions of Americans losing their  jobs – 10.8% unemployment in 2008, and millions of Americans having their homes foreclosed. Enter Democrat Obama to rescue Bush II's  Depression reframed as  "Recession".-- the Dow Jones dropped from 14,164 in the fall of 2007 to 6,500 in 2009. and unemployment of10.2% in 2009, down to 4.9% under Obama in December 2015. (Trump deceived, lied, and propagandized that all that Obama did in eight years to rescue Americans from Dubya's two wars of self-indulgence and his Not-So Great-Depression," which caused millions of Americans to lose their jobs and homes, was solely due to Trump's three years of giving to his rich confederates that which made them richer, and taking from the poor so they would become poorer.) And Trump's Depression of 2020, was caused in significant part by Trump's refusal to admit to the Covid—19 pandemic, and take appropriate steps to combat it

Democrat Clinton ended the Bosnian War, Republican Dubya illegally started the War in Afghanistan, falsely claiming the Taliban was the direct and proximate cause of the 9/11 attacks by providing cover for some 2,000 – 3,000 al- Qaeda high-jackers responsible  for the 9/11 attacks on New York's Twin Towers and the Pentagon, when Bush knew, or should have known 15 of the 38 high-jackers were Saudi nationals, all of whom avoided retaliation by Bush due to the close personal relationship between the House of Bush oil and  Saudi royalty-oil House.

Next, wimpy, wartime deserter Dubya Bush, now Commander of Chief, needing a wussy foreign leader to vanquish, turns loose a propaganda blitzkrieg of lies that Saddam Hussein, who Poppy Bush defeated in 100 hours, is now murdering his own women and children with biological and chemical weapons, and must be "taken out."  (No such weapons were found.

Nineteen years later the war still goes on – 10,000 Americans killed in Dubya's phony war to out-duel Poppy Bush.

Democrat Obama tried to end both of Dubya's unwinnable wars, yet global bully, and five deferments, Trump, whose father paid a podiatrist to find a non-existent spur on Donald's foot so Donald could avoid serving his country in the Vietnam War, itching for a fight, first insults North Korea's leader, provokes Iran by unleashing the dogs of war on its territorial waters, and threatens to invade Venezuela.

Indeed Trump, motivated by the same narcissistic delusion of omnipotence as Dubya looks around for his Saddam Hussein, but finds only

Germany's Merkek, France's Macron, and Canada's Trudeau to insult, provoke, and bully.

As for Russia's Putin, Trump, realizes he is no match for Putin – can't beat him, so he joins him in sharing the world's stage.

For his part, Putin sees  advantage in the United States electing an ingratiating, easily manipulated, mentally disturbed, paper tiger, Besides, Putin has a score to settle against Hillary Clinton, who had challenged Putin in the past.

The Trump-Putin Alliance – not about nuclear weapons, rather all about getting Trump elected and Hillary defeated, unleashes a two-front, social media propaganda feeding frenzy in which Trump leads his frenetic rally chanting "Killer Hillary," absent any mention that Trump, soon to be  the Commander in Chief,  had committed felony fraud to avoid serving his country in its Vietnam War.

It worked on both counts."

Brody;"Your Honor, the Prosecution protests in the strongest way possible! The Defendant's dilatory stalling tactics have long ago wandered so far from an argument as to jurisdiction that I must move this Court that the Defendant's entire random and irrelevant statement be stricken,and his motion for recusal and his motion for  alternative jurisdiction be dismissed as trivial and frivolous."

Dr. Otis: "I acknowledge  the Prosecutor's eagerness to get his hanging, but I must temper his distemper by showing this Court that first Bush II and then Trump I's takeover of the Federal courts, which "trickles down" to state and local courts, promises partial outcomes to Conservative causes and

unfavorable outcomes to causes antithetical to
Conservative dogma and doxology, the current case at
bar being but a notorious example of the latter.

In fact, I ask this Court to consider that Trump's
coup of the Federal judiciary – two Conservative
Supreme Court Judges in  only 34 months, when it took
Obama eight years to seat two Supreme Court judges,
and Trump, along with malevolent Senate leader
McConnell, obstructed justice and conspired to obstruct
justice by refusing to vote on Obama's constitutional
right to appoint Merrick Garland to the US Supreme
Court, in order to have Trump appoint a Conservative
judge – Gorsuch – is indicative of how quickly Trump
morphed from President elected in January 2016, to
Unholy American Emperor in 2020 – from Capitalism's
Prodigal Son to Conservative Republican Party's
Frankenstein monster. (It took Hitler from 1918 to 1933
to be elected Germany's President, but less than one
year for Trump to be elected, albeit a back-door
President of the United States.

In Hitler's defense, Trump had the advantage of
leftovers – victims of Conservative Republican
President Bush II's 2007 economic meltdown, the
legacy of the Old South's, die-hard, white, Supremacist
males, sore losers still convinced their Southern Baptist
God gave his blessing to slavery.

Hitler also didn't have FOX News – a pox on
any non-totalitarian regime, in the case of the United
States, another instance of Conservatives' perverse
reading of the 'free speech" Constitutional provision as
licensing lies, slander, and extremist Conservative
propaganda as "news." with no requirement that equal
time (free speech) be given to opposing viewpoints,

thus making false folk heroes of professional liars like Loose Lips Limbaugh, Pope O'Reilly, Harried Haranguing Hannity, Mucker "Man Without Conscience" Carlson, and TV evangelists – psychopaths – every one.

Hitler also didn't have the added advantage of a population whose public education had been underfunded by Republicans and Conservatives for generations. (Reagan even tried to abolish the Department of Education

Trump's DeVos is trying to do the same, all resulting in today's legion oflazy-brainedTrumpists too "uneducated," too illiterate, with too low IQ'sto distinguish between fact and Trump's fiction – his lies, his propaganda,  thereby denying me a jury of my peers– another reason to deny me my Fourteenth Amendment right to equal protection under the laws."

Brody: "Your Honor, the Defendant's profane re-ordering of history aside, I must again respectfully request – demand -- that the Defendant's entire dissertation of the disturbed be stricken as irrelevant, made in bad faith – a shoddy delaying tactic --"

Dr. Otis: "To the contrary, what is more relevant than a defendant's Fourteenth Amendment right to a fair and impartial adjudication of his defense guaranteed by the Constitution of the United States, and what is more fundamental to that guarantee than a unbiased judge, a neutral and competent jury of my peers, and a social/political milieu committed to the truth and the Bill of Rights?

Trump, having eluded multiple criminal indictments via the Mueller Report's bogus excuse "sitting presidents are above the law," and having avoided impeachment due to treasonous Republican Senators voting Conservative Republican Party over country, kept right on excessively abusing his  power and authority by willfully, maliciously, and criminally, stalling his intervention to the COVID -19 pandemic, causing Americans to die, inciting states to open too soon, causing more Americans to die, exploiting the national protests against racial injustice and the police murder of George Floyd, to divide the Country for his personal political gain, ordering federal troops to invade Democratic cities under the ruse to protect government buildings from protesters, when the sole lawless purpose was to incite protesters to riot against Trump's *Gestapo,* so Trump could then anoint himself as the new "law and order, President, thereby rescuing his presidential campaign form the crapper.

One of Trump's most flagrant assaults on my 14th Amendment right to a fair and  impartial hearing and my equal protection under the laws, was Trump's unconstitutional, unethical, conspiratorial acts with Senate Whip  McConnell and Senate Republicans to: (1) Illegally refuse to vote on Obama's proper nomination of Merrick Garland for the Supreme Court in 2016,  to fill the vacancy due to the death of Antonin Scalia,  (2) Violate my  Constitutional right to a fair and impartial  hearing of my defense, by nominating Neil Gorsuch as Supreme Court Judge for the sole purpose of establishing a Conservatively biased Court, (3) Violate my Constitutional right to a fair and impartial hearing of my defense, by nominating Bret "I love beer and drunk women" Kavanaugh as Supreme Court Judge for the sole purpose of establishing a Conservatively biased Court, (4) Violate my Constitutional right to a fair and impartial  hearing of my defense, by illegally, criminally, and unconstitutionally stacking the United States Supreme Court with Conservatively biased Judges who will vote for Conservative causes and against liberal/progressive causes.(5)  Violate my Constitutional right to a fair and impartial  hearing of my defense, by nominating only Conservatively biased Article III Federal Judges (197) and 51, (record number) Court of Appeal Judges., thereby violating the fundamental promise to every American of a fair and impartial judiciary,'

Trump, having so poisoned the courts to render all liberal *progressive* cases and causes DOA, similarly corrupted the social/cultural milieu with his divisive, morally bankrupt, depraved, mean-spirited, evil, to wit, Executive Orders, policy statements/pronouncements, and Tweets as  to turn fathers against sons, neighbors against neighbors, Conservatives against non-Conservatives, South against  North, White supremacists /Neo -Nazis against humanists, old world immigrants against new world immigrants, Conservatives against Liberals, Church against State, blue states against red states, rich against poor. America against its allies,  Friends of foes made, – a house divided  by virulence and vindictiveness,  not seen since Reconstruction – the landlord being a severely mentally disordered troll deluded he is better than everyone else in the world when the reality is quite the opposite.

Trump's  coupd'état being both the direct cause of my alleged actions in this case and why this Court must provide with due diligence the proper jurisdiction for a fair and impartial adjudication promised me by the Constitution of the United States.

Such deliberations must include a review of those specific acts by Bush II and Trump I, which has so poisoned, prejudiced, and divided the American public as to make seating a fair and impartial jury in this case, mission impossible.

For example, while, Mr. Bush II's egregious narcissistic sins – (1) two illegal unwinnable wars still being fought nearly 20 years later, which killed 10,000 Americans and (2) Bush II's deregulated banks and mortgage companies which short-circuited Wall Street costing millions of Americans to lose their homes and jobs. while Bush immediately rushed to bail out these same banks, whose greed caused the Depression, with a $700 billion bailout to "rescue Wall Street," but not a dime to rescue the millions on Main Street, now enraged –  furious with the Government rather than  the true villains – Conservative Republican bankers and Conservative Republican mortgage companies, who in 2016, became easy prey to Trump's treachery and fraud that they should blame Obama and Hillary and trust Trump as their Lord and savior, as described in my book, *Trump's Troops Revolt Against Republican Party's Betrayal,*

Eight years later, second Narcissistic Personality Disorder, Trump, whose love  and devotion of himself erupted into a confluence of narcissistic "high crimes and misdemeanors" including, but not limited to castrating President Obama's  presidency by attacking Obama's Affordable Care Act, rescinding President Obama's equal pay rule, quashing Obama's Order prohibiting states from withholding family planning funding from organizations performing abortions and other reproductive health services, and voiding

Obama's plan not to renew contracts for private companies running  prisons reasoning private companies  produce no better results  but at a greater cost.

Trump withdrew the United States from Obama's Trans-Pacific Partnership, from the Paris Agreement signed by Obama and194 other countries, withdrew the US from the Iran-Nuclear Deal, strongly backed by President Obama, rescinded President Obama's Order offering temporary residency to undocumented children whose parents were already legally residing in the US, rescinded President Obama's guidelines allowing transgenders to serve in the military, and rescinded President Obama's banning the transfer of military-style weapons to local police to avoid people feeling as though they were under military occupation, rather than being protected by local police in the community. Trump reversed Obama's policy protecting transgender workers. Trump reversed President Obama's birth control mandate limiting employers denying birth control to employees on moral or religious grounds. Trump rescinded President Obama's guidelines for investigating college sexual assault complaints, rescinded President Obama's protection for transgender students in public schools, and rescinded President Obama's "net neutrality" regulations thereby giving some service providers "most favored status" over others. Trump reversed President Obama's opposition to the "global gag rule" which orders that all foreign organizations receiving US global assistance are forbidden to provide abortion services, or to counsel patients about abortion services. Trump reversed President Obama's opposition to the

Keystone Pipeline, which Obama had objected to on Native American and environmental concerns, and Trump reversed President Obama's policy of avoiding charging non-violent  drug offenders with crimes that required mandatory sentencing. Trump lowered Obama's nutritional standards for school lunches, diluted President Obama's clean water regulations  and deregulated over 20 President Obama's environmental standards and regulations, calling climate change a "hoax". Trump promised voters he would repeal and replace Obamacare – The Affordable Care Act, but despite his efforts  to starve Obamacare by cutting funding, Trump has failed to either repeal or replace Obamacare. Trump has attempted to undermine Medicaid by requiring work as a precondition to receiving medical insurance.

The Dodd-Frank Law was implemented to prevent the bank and mortgage companies from causing another Bush llDepression, and gave rise to the Consumer Protection Bureau.

Trump appointed Mulvaney the Director of the Budget in charge of the Consumer Protection Agency, which Mulvaney had promised to trash. Trump torpedoed Obama's attempts to normalize relations with Cuba. Trump. appointed agency secretaries based on their sworn loyalty to Trump, not to the  Republic and its citizens, and their history of excoriating the very agency they were to head.

For example Trump's Secretary of Education DeVos, former Chairperson of the Michigan Republican Party and billionaire, who never had a degree in education, never attended public schools, never sent her children to public schools, never worked in a school setting, is outspoken in her bias for alternatives to public schools, unconstitutionally awarding vouchers to church and charter schools, yet Trump put her in charge of America's public schools and colleges.

Trump appointed Bill Barr to be Attorney General, withholding information from the public that Barr had made a $2,700 donation to Trump's 2016 campaign, that Barr viewed the US presidency in general, and Trump's reign as "Donald the Deity," as he did his Catholic Pope – infallible and who, like America's late Pope Scalia, Barr's first loyalty is to the Roman Catholic Church. Barr had called Mueller's investigation as to Trump's acts  of obstruction of justice" asinine," and characterized Mueller's Report as "entirely a political operation to overthrow the president," yet, 400 of our best and brightest legal experts determined that except for the Justice Department's self-serving policy of not charging a sitting president of crimes, Trump would have been convicted for multiple crimes of Obstruction of Justice – all of which leads to one conclusion: Trump's appointment of Barr as Attorney General was itself a criminal act to obstruct justice, and Trump, Barr, and the Republican Senators who voted to confirm Barr, must as a matter of law, be charged with criminally conspiring to obstruct justice, Department of Justice Policy be damned and condemned as conflict of interests.

.Trump appointed bloodthirsty, trigger-happy, warmongering John Bolton as National Security Adviser/*de facto* Secretary of Defense who, like Bush II joined the National Guard for the sole purpose of avoiding active duty in Vietnam and who, just like Dubya, never spent a day fighting for his country, while sending other American soldiers to die, with the missionary zeal of a Southern Baptist waiting to kill a doctor entering an abortion clinic.

Shortly thereafter, unable to control Bolton, Trump claims to have fired him, only to even later excoriate and slander Bolton for his "tell all book" exposing Trump as an incompetent, self-indulgent, erratic president who often broke the rules and laws to gain political and personal advantage.

The point being that Trump, like Dubya before him, was so disabled by his Narcissistic Personality Disorder that his every presidential act was an outward manifestation of his delusion that he was the "greatest president ever" – that every word from his mouth, or written in his tweets, is *ex cathedra* true, and every Trump action hailed as if it were the word of a god.

So it was that Trump, true to his delusion of riding co-pilot with the Christian God, conned, coerced, and defrauded the victims of Dubya's Depression – those who understood nothing beyond headlines, bumper-stickers, slick TV preachers and Divine Donald's sermons on Twitter – tweets from the White House -- to Trumps "red hats,' like Hitler's brown-shirts – eager to war for  Trump, who promised to get their jobs back, when that is the constitutional function of Congress, not Trump, who, having taken credit for the job increase 2016-2019,  must now take responsibility for the 30- 40 MILLION American jobs lost in February 2020, to the present , caused by Trump, who claims to be "the greatest president ever."

In any event, the evidence is compelling and inexorable: Trump's*de facto* Neo-Nazi Conservative takeover of the Republic, the  federal, state, and local judiciary, the US Supreme Court, the Republican Party, the US Senate, federal governmental agencies, particularly the Department of Justice and its crooked Attorney General, the national media via FOX News, the military, trade, treaties, tariffs, war, national defense, law enforcement, prisons, public education, guns, education, and immigrants – Trump, like Bush II, divides Americans as "friend" – all those swearing allegiance to Divined Despot Donald J. Trump, and "foe' – all those who swear allegiance to the United States of America, thereby decreasing my chances of a fair and impartial judge and jury to 38%!

A reasonable and prudent person, convinced by the evidence herein presented above,  that a fair and impartial adjudication of my defense is not possible within the borders of the United Sates and its territories, I move that the Court petition the International Court of Justice, under exceptional circumstances, to hear this case, or in the alternative, that the Court seek jurisdiction by the International Court of Justice, which accepts jurisdiction of "contentious issues." of which this case certainly qualifies."

Judge Vance, looking at the Courtroom clock, announces, "This Court stands adjourned.

## Day Two

Judge Vance, upon taking his seat on the bench, announces," As to the Defendant's motion that I recuse myself under 28 US. Code #455(a), the Defendant has failed to show unto this Court that my having been appointed by the younger President George  Bush, is insufficient *prima facie* grounds for my recusal. Therefore the Defendant's motion that I recuse myself is denied."

Dr. Otis; "Objection. Your stated grounds for dismissal appear to be based on a misapprehension of my argument for recusal, to wit, I did not contend that my motion for recusal was based on the fact that you were appointed by Bush II, but was rather due to you having been nominated for the judgeship because you were, as was ex-President Bush, first and foremost, a card-carrying Conservative.

Stated differently, without Conservative credentials you would not have been nominated, meaning your appointment was not to preserve, protect and defend the Constitution of the United States, as was your sworn duty, but rather to preserve, protect, and defend Conservative causes *uber alles* – be a militant money-makes- right Christian soldier for Neo-Conservative causes wherever that battle may be fought – the Constitutional Republic, the American body politic, and its citizens be damned!

One such battle recently fought by Ultra-Conservative Neo-Nazi, Antonin  Scalia, whose malicious, treasonous, and fraudulent misapprehension of the Second Amendment, in *Columbia v. Heller,* declared the right tobear arms applies to individuals defending themselves, when Scalia knew, Conservatives and the NRA knew, Scalia had criminally and maliciously omitted the first 13 words of the Second Amendment, to wit, "A well-regulated militia, being necessary to the security of a free state ..."

The meaning is clear, certain, and compelling
The Second Amendment applies to citizens being able
to grab their musket from over the mantle to join his
neighbors in defense of their "free state,"-- America
against  foreign foe – Britain.
No mention is stated, nor implied in the Second
Amendment as to individuals having the right to bear
arms of any kind to protect himself or herself against
another individual.
He/she may well have that right to bear arms
against his neighbor, but he must establish that right by
some other law or statute, NOT the Second
Amendment.
White Supremacists, Neo-Nazi thugs, and
males, particularly in the South, fearing oppressed and
vocationally castrated African-American males night do
another Nat Turner, justify their paranoia, by
fraudulently claiming the Second Amendment allows
them to bear – carry- brandish  assault weapons  into
church and the marketplace,
Gutless politicians like deceased Antonin Scalia,
fearing losing the support of the NRA, rabidly vote
Conservative and Republican, thus capitulating to the
NRA and their fraudulent  bogus argument that the
Second Amendment grants citizens the right to bears
arms against their neighbor or individuals.
In another  recent example of the Neo-
Conservative US Supreme Court judges failing their
sworn duty to preserve, protect, and defend  the
Constitution also occurred under the command of Ultra-
Conservative Neo-Nazi, Supreme Court Judge Antonin

Scalia, who, by means of malicious, treasonous, and fraudulent misapprehension of the First  Amendment right to free-speech, ruled in *Citizens United v. FEC,* "… that the government is prohibited from limiting individual expenditures – money, or their equivalent, as to political speech."  (That same Conservative United States Supreme Court having fraudulently ruled Corporations are individuals, when the Conservative judges knew, or should have known, corporations were conceived to shield the individual business owner who would otherwise be liable for defective products, deceptive business practices, and labor abuses.

By now fraudulently ruling in *Citizens United* that corporations were back being individuals, the late Conservative Pope Scalia and his confederate judges kept the corporate owners' shield against liability in place, while at the same time, allowing them as individuals to make unlimited monetary contributions – bribes – to politicians, in turn guaranteeing Conservative Republican corporate owners  control the government –'He who pays the Piper, controls the tune,' meaning government -- always the 'closet' wind-up toy for the *nouveau riche* – now "outed," admitted to being the government "of, for, and by the capitalists."

The "one man one vote rule," always a myth, was openly voided by *Citizens United.* Oh, he/she could vote – unless he/she was non-white, could not produce a photo ID, was a felon, (Where in the Constitution does it take the right to vote away from anyone?), or was without transportation to the polls.

Even so, his /her vote would have zero influence against the *Citizens United* National Rifle Association million dollar donations – bribes – which would now openly decide who was elected and who was defeated.

The lust for money being the cause of all evil, America became Reagan's "evil empire. "by way of Scalia's*Citizens United* treasonous travesty.

Judge Vance: "This Court is unmoved. The Defendant's  motion to recuse is denied. Case closed!"

Dr. Otis: "Are you denying that by reason of being appointed federal judge by Conservative President Bush II because you were first and foremost a member of the Federalists wing of the Conservative Party" –

Judge Vance: There is no Conservative Party" –

Dr. Otis: "There is now due to Trump's coup of the Republican Party in the name of Neo-Nazi Conservatives,."

Judge Vance; "Your Motion to recuse is denied."

Dr. Otis: "28 US. Code #455(a) states, 'Any judge or magistrate judge of the United States shall disqualify himself in any proceeding in which his impartiality might reasonably be questioned ... Any circumstance in which a judge's impartiality might reasonably be questioned under § 455 (a) requires disqualification, even if the circumstance is not enumerated as in § 455(b) … When the impartiality of a judge is in doubt, the appropriate remedy is to disqualify that judge from hearing further proceedings in the matter."

Judge Vance: "I need not be reminded of the law by a *pro se* litigant."

Dr. Otis: "And by that statement you commit yet another act of bias, this time against *pro se* litigants."

Judge Vance: "Your motion to recuse is denied. Case dismissed."

Brody: "At this time, the Prosecution would like to make its Opening Statement, Your Honor."

Dr. Otis: "Are you going to plead to the US Court of Appeals  that having been appointed by Conservative President Bush II, who you and I both know would not have appointed you unless your conservatism met the litmus test of Conservative purity, you nevertheless can now administer this trial without your conservative partiality being  reasonably questioned under § 455 (a), thereby denying me due process right to an impartial adjudication– exposing me to an "outward manifestation of what could reasonably be construed as bias" leading to consequences so dire – a death sentence – that disqualification is required, *United States v. Bobo*."

Judge Vance: "The Prosecution may make its Opening Statement;"

Dr. Otis: "What of my motion for a change of venue?"

Judge Vance; "Denied"

Dr. Otis: "On what basis/"

Judge Vance: "Frivolous."

Dr. Otis: "Frivolous?  Compelling evidence that I cannot get a fair trial in the United States because Trump's Reign Of Hate and Divisiveness has so poisoned the body politic that a fair and impartial jury of my peers is impossible, is frivolous?"

Judge Vance: "The prosecution may now make its Opening Statement."

Dr. Otis; "Exception. I am herein advising the Court I will Appeal."

Judge Vance: "Duly noted. Bailiff, you may seat the Jury".

Brody: "Members of the jury, let me begin by thanking you for performing this thankless task of civic duty by serving on this jury. Without you and the thousands of jurors before you, there would be no courts, no system of justice, and no democracy. Again, on behalf of all your fellow American citizens, I thank you.

It is a well-settled fact among lawyers and judges that no case is a slam dunk. It is also part of legal lore that for every rule there are three exceptions. Both hold true as far as the case before you is concerned.

Please let me explain. First, this case is a slam dunk due to the fact that the Defendant does not deny that he murdered the President of the United States,DonaldJ.Trump. Second we are here today only because  the Defendant, now faced with the reality of a lethal injection, wants us to make an exception for him by changing our definition of the word "murder."

You may recall another instance in which a President of the United States tried to convince us of his innocence – a much more innocuous offense I assure you-- by redefining a word  – that time the word was "sex," not murder.

We weren't fooled then, we won't be fooled now.

I know it's easy to forget, with all the tedious and trifling cognitive dissonant ramblings from the Defendant, but the Judge did remind you that18 U.S. Code #1111, defines "murder" as the unlawful killing of a human being with malice of aforethought–planned in advance – predicated is murder in the first degree to be punished by death or by imprisonment for life. 18 U.S. Code 1757 # IIII specifically lists causing the death of the President of the United States is a capital offense for which the death sentence must be imposed.

So there you have it – a slam dunk! For murdering President Trump,, the Defendant has all but put the needle in his own arm.

The Defendant does not dispute the fact that he caused the death of President Trump, but rather than murder, the Defendant would have you believe that he acted in defense of the United States.

I know from the looks on your faces that you find the Defendant's argument incredible. I agree. But in our system of justice,, the accused is presumed innocent until  proven  guilty in a court of law by a jury of his peers and that everyone has a First Amendment right to his or her day in court..

So we come together today at this time in history and at this place, to render a judgment as to the Defendant's guilt or innocence as to the charge, under 18 U.S. Code #IIII – First Degree Murder of the President of the United States, one Donald J. Trump.

As you may have also recalled, the Defendant tried, but failed, to get his Honorable Judge Vance to recuse – remove himself from the case, on the specious grounds that the Honorable Judge Vance would not offer him a fair and impartial Hearing simply because

President Bush, a Republican, appointed him judge, as opposed to the Defendant, a Democrat to the left of radical Socialist Sanders.

Not only did Judge Vance dismiss the Defendant's frivolous motion to recuse – remove himself – causing the Defendant to incur the same Judge Vance's displeasure the Defendant had claimed was grounds for the Judge to recuse himself! Self-fulfilling prophecy, wouldn't you agree/?

In addition, due to his bad judgment, the Defendant risked antagonizing you, his jurors, who as representatives, by definition, of the general citizenry, view judges with reverence, just below that of rabbis and pastors and just above that of their doctor. By subverting that reverence each of you bestows on your judges – Judge Vance in particular, being center stage, the Defendant inherits the role as "bad guy"  before the first shot is fired from the witness stand.

The Defendant's first attempt to get Judge Vance removed from this case failed, so the Defendant tries a new scheme, this time claiming that because President Trump was so popularthe Defendant could not  receive a fair trial anywhere in the United States.

Therefore, the case must be removed to the International Criminal Court in the Hague, Netherlands, which the Defendant knew could never happen because the United States never ratified its membership, thereby rendering  the transfer impossible, even if this Court ruled the transfer take place which the Defendant knew would never happen due to President Bush's refusal to join arguing, "American's interests would be unfairly treated for political reasons."

Next, using the same specious argument, the
Defendant tried to persuade Judge Vance to move the
case to the International Court of Justice, aka, the
World Court, also in the Hague, Netherlands.

The Defendant is deluded that while
his despicable and egregious crime  of  murdering the
President of the United States  ripples throughout the
world, the issues involved – the Defendant, acted alone,
not as a member of any foreign or domestic
organization, not as a  terrorist, instead motivated by
personal reasons of no public, and certainly of no
international implication or reverberations, failed to
meet the jurisdictional standards of the World Court.

Therefore, absent grounds for Judge Vance to
dismiss his motion for a change of venue to the Hague,
notwithstanding the fact that the United States has
never surrendered its sovereign immunity to
International tribunals since the Nuremberg Trials, the
Defendant's motion for a change of Venue was
properly dismissed.

If it seems to you as it does to me that the
Defendant suddenly awoke to the reality that the
Government of the United States, with your help, was
going to put the needle of death in his arm unless he
could concoct some cockamamie,  way of getting Judge
Vance to recuse – remove himself as if the Defendant
could remove judges *ad infinitum* until he found  one
appointed by a Democratic President – and when that
ploy was dismissed, the Defendant tried two equally
frivolous and laughable motions for a change of venue,
first to The International Court of Justice, of which the
United States is not a member, and then to the
International Court of Justice , aka, the World Court,

deluded that the World Court would be persuaded to hear a case of in which the Defendant assassinated the President of the United States.

Now, the Defendant's chutzpah out of the way, and his guilt established, let us consider motive, and for that, we look to others who have also assassinated the President. to the United  States.

On April 14, 1865,stage actor John Wilkes Booth, made his way into the Ford Theater here in Washington, where President Lincoln was watching a production of "My American Cousin" from a box on the second floor, with his wife.

Booth snuck up behind Lincoln and shot him in the head. Lincoln died the next morning.

Booth was one of several Confederate sympathizers who had plotted to kill President Lincoln. and two other members of his cabinet that night,

Booth hid in a barn, which was torched by Union forces, who shot Booth as he fled the fire.

The other members of the conspiracy were hanged.

On July 2, 1881,Charles Guiteau, lawyer and professor, whose father opined that Charles was possessed by Satan, having had his application for Ambassador of France personally rejected by President Garfield, shot  Garfield at short range, and was hung for his crime.

September 6,1901, Leon Czolgosz, alleged anarchist, who had lost his job in the "Panic" of 1893, apparently blamed President McKinley for the "Panic" and as being an enemy of "good working people,"

Czolgosz shot McKinley twice in the stomach as McKinley was greeting the public at the Pan-

American Exposition in Buffalo, NY on September 6, 1901, and died on September 14<sup>th</sup>.

Czolgosz was electrocuted.

Democrat President John F. Kennedy was ambushed and killed by Lee Harvey Oswald on Friday November 22, 1963 at 12:30 P.M, as Kennedy was riding in an open car in a presidential motorcade as it passed through Dealey Plaza in Dallas, Texas

Oswald was subsequently killed by Jack Ruby as Oswald was in police custody, thereby leaving the world to speculate as to why Oswald killed Kennedy.

Dr. Diamond, a psychologist, reasoned Oswald, whose father died before Oswald was born, made Oswald feel less a man , and more a Mommy's boy' – Oswald slept in his mother's bed before turning 12 – had a compulsion to do something real big to make him seem a real man on the world's stage. – what :bigger thing to do than to assassinate the President of the United State, John Kennedy?.

June 6, 1968, SirhanSirhan, a 24 year-old Palestinian, pulled a .22 pistol from a campaign program and killed Robert Kennedy as he was making his way through a crowd celebrating his California primary win at the Los Angeles  Ambassador Hotel.

Kennedy died the next morning.     There was no death penalty in California, so Sirhan was given a life sentence.

His reason for killing Kennedy was because of Kennedy's alleged support of Israel in the 1967 Six Days War. and Kennedy's alleged "oppression of the Palestinians."

April 4, 1968, while Martin Luther King was standing on the second story balcony of the  Lorraine

Motel in Memphis, Tennessee, James Earl Ray, from the bathroom window of a boarding house across the street, fired a single shot from his .30-06 rifle into the head of 39 year-old Martin Luther King. (Ray had bought the rifle and scope  just a few days earlier,

In his rush to abscond, Ray left his rifle and binoculars at the scene, and fled in his Mustang to Canada where he got a passport under  a different name, flew to England, where he was recognized and arrested at the Heathrow Airport in London.

Ray, the oldest of 9 children, and son of a father with a prison record, quit school at age 15, and until he died in prison in 1998 of liver failure, had begun his criminal career in 1949 for robbery, one year after being  dishonorably discharged from the Army. In 1959, while on parole, Ray received a 20 year sentence for armed robbery of two grocery stores, He escaped in1967, by hiding in a bakery truck making delivery to the prison. He fled to Mexico where he had his face changed and sold himself as a porn film director. He returned to the States, where he volunteered to help arch- segregationist/white supremacist George Wallace's presidential campaign, and in March, 1968, Raybought  the rifle, scope, and ammunition he used to kill Martin Luther King a few days later.

Ray's motive was the same as that of thousands of southern white males in 1968, who were threatened by civil rights in general, and the resulting upward mobility of the African-American male, who prior to 1968, was assigned automatic status below that of the worst of the "white trash" – the Bob Ewells of *To kill a Mockingbird* .

Our review of those who assassinated American Presidents or those with the status of presidents, would be remiss if we failed to note those who tried, but failed, to wit, John Hinckley, who tried, but only wounded our President  Reagan, out of some perverted plan to win the heart of Jodie Foster.

Lynette "Sqeaky" Fromm, and member of the Charles Manson cult, who in protest against the effect of pollution  on the air, trees, water, and animals, on September 5, 1975, while but an arm's length away from President Ford, pulled the trigger on her M1911 pistol, which didn't fire because she had forgotten to put the bullet in the chamber.

She served 34 years of a life sentence, and was released on 8/14/09.

Sarah Jane Moore, who, 15 days later, on September 20, 1975, fired her .38 at President Ford from 40 feet away, but missed, because she failed to adjust the sight on the gun she had just bought. She too was given a life sentence served 32 and was released in 2007.

In retrospect Moore opined, "I was blinded by political views.:
Confederate zealot, McKinley's Czolosz an underclass warrior,  King's Ray a Confederate white supremacist, Robert Kennedy's Sirhan a Palestinian defender, Ford's "Squeaky' Fromm a tree-hugging radical, and Ford's Moore, "blinded by my political views."

The other group of presidential assassins and almost presidential assassins – psychological/mentally deranged – includes Garfield's Guiteau, a rejected job seeker as ambassador to France,  Oswald, who believed the assassination of JFK would make him the man the death of his father before Oswald was born  and, Reagan's  Hinckley a wannabe lover who would never be.

The prosecution will show you, the jury, that the Defendant belongs to both groups -- a political assassin who referred to President Trump's nationalism as Neo-Nazism, which can only be disposed of by getting rid of – murdering assassinating President Trump, and psychological/mental defect or disease -- the Defendant's obsessive hatred of President Trump drove him to plan killing President Trump from day President Trump  took his oath of Office.

I have here in my hand two books written by the Defendant – One titled "Why And  How We The People Must  Remove Trump." – "remove" meaning get rid of – assassinate, where you will read –  see for yourselves, in the Defendants own words, his stated reasons for assassinating President Trump, and  the other book, "Trump's Troops Revolt Against Republican Party's Betrayal," – the Prosecution's double-barrel smoking gun – the Defendant's written admission of his guilt.

I suppose, in a quirky way, you and I should be grateful to the Defendant for having made our job of finding him guilty of the premeditated assassination of the President of the United States Donald J. Trump, so easy.

Together, we will have our justice, for ourselves, our children, our  grandchildren, our fellow Americans, and the world.

Thank you."

Judge Vance: "The Defendant may now make his Opening Statement.

Prosecutor Brody: "Your Honor, Must we give the Defendant two bites of the apple, when the Defendant has already eaten the
 all but the core of the first one?'

Judge Vance: "Haste and justice share a mutual distrust, as well they should. You may proceed Mr. Otis.'

Dr. Otis: "Thank you Judge for both your homily and your permission to proceed…

Persons of the jury, please indulge me as to my understanding as to how the prosecutor and defendant are to conduct their respective business.

First, the prosecutor 's role, is, as is the job of Fox News, to propagandize Conservatism as the one true ism *uber alles,* the sole arbiter of all truths and knowledge and mortal enemy of any dissenter or worse, a non-Conservative – conservatism being a secular religion of zealots of no less fanaticism and intolerance than that of ISIS, who, by virulent slander, defamation of my character, treacherous assaults on my very being – the most unconscionable lies to  portray me as the penultimate villain-- despicable, satanic and most murderous subhuman since Satan himself, (Leaving the implausible existence of a Satan for another forum), while the defense attorney's job is to lie in kind – convince the jury that his client is slightly less than Saint Francis of Assisi but sitting at the right hand of the local pastor – a person who could not have possibly committed the crime as alleged,  all of which renders justice a game of chance played in a courthouse instead of a casino.

The Prosecutor's opening statement provides clear and compelling evidence he chooses the "best lie wins," *modus operandi.*

He has precedent, but not morality, not ethics, and certainly not  integrity on his side.

As you will ascertain for yourselves, that like you, I am neither Satan nor Savior, neither murderer nor minister, neither Sirhan nor Oswald.

I did that which any one of you would have done had you concluded as I did, that my country to which, as a young boy, I had pledged allegiance every morning in school, saluted its flag, honored its commitment as a republic – not a democracy – nowhere in the Declaration of Independence, nor the Constitution is a democracy stated or implied.

The beloved United States of my youth is now a house re-divided – or as John Dean so aptly described it – a "broken government" –  or as Kevin Phillips' book describes –An *American Theocracy,* or as I might add, a Capitalistic Conservative, evangelical Oligarchy run by a deliberate  dysfunctional Congress with its Southern Republican Senators still subversive traitors in the service of the Confederacy – so called Red State conservative politicians taking control of all federal and state governmental agencies – demonizing the federal government,  but being first in line to collect federal dollars for floods, fires, droughts, and hurricanes. Corporate CEO's dictating state and federal policy-- the NRA bribing Scalia's Supreme Court to fraudulently rule the Second Amendment guarantees the individual the right to bear arms to protect against other individuals, when the Second Amendment grants no such right – rather the right to bear arms, "being necessary to the security of a free State," to join with one's neighbors to protect the free State (the United States) against enemies, foreign or domestic.

The result of the NRA/ Conservative Scalia US Supreme Court's conspiratorial fraud, America's schools run red in the blood of children killed by deranged individuals bearing arms provided by the NRA. while every day America's Nero, Tweets while America implodes -- victims of his Narcissistic Reign of Delusions of Grandeur.

But you say, the Republic will be saved by the ballot box, to which I say, not when the ballot box is controlled by Trump's Tweets, not while he Trump tries to rig the election by disenfranchising the US Postal Service, his daily propaganda blitzkrieg of national and social media, FOX News – Conservative propaganda 24/7, under the fraudulent veil of "free speech," a friendly Conservative FAA, the Hitleresque rantings of "Haranguing Hannity" and Loose Lips Limbaugh.-- all *summa cum laude* graduates of Goebbels' Politics 101: "Tell the lies as often as necessary until the masses believe the lies to be true."

In that same context, it is worth noting that Trump's Red Hats" threaten force to enforce Trumpism as did Hitler's brown shirts enforce Nazism.

You ask, "How is your justification any different than that of Booth, Czolgosz, Ray, Sirhan, Fromm, or More, who the Prosecutor describes  as having assassinated presidents for political reasons?"

Fair enough. The difference is that my assessment of Trump's threat to America and Americans represents the calculations of  the majority of Americans, when Booth, Czolgosz, Ray, Sirhan,

Fromm, or More, were personal and private grievances voidof a consensus.

In fact, it was the very numbers of experts who believed as I did , and before I did, that allowed me to expect that Trump would be removed by Amendment 25, Section 4 which
requires that the vice-president and the cabinet must agree that the President is no longer able, or fit to be President -- Mission Impossible– Vice-President Pence was Trump's wind-up toy – his lap dog, a mannequin of a man and Trump's cabinet hand-picked by Trump to do as Trump demanded or be fired -- too afraid, too timid,  too subservient and too devoid of conscience or character to ever displease

Ok, then the Mueller Report would save the Republic from Trump's ruinous reign of self-imposed delusions of grandeur.

Not likely when Republican Conservative foot-soldier Mueller, owned and controlled by Trump's puppet Attorney General Barr , who, in decreed that Department of Justice policy,-- not rule or law -- but now etched in stone, that a sitting president could not be charged with a crime – lawless Trump was above the law!

Impeachment them! Even less likely .The treasonous Republican Senators by reason of voting Party over Country, lead by Public Enemy Number Two– Old South racist Mitch McConnell, the Senate hit man, who once announced that making Obama a "one-term president"  was his top priority, regardless of whatever good Obama might do for the Country, and who himself should have been impeached for violating the Constitution  for refusing to vote on Obama's

nomination  for the Supreme Court vacancy for the sole
malicious purpose of giving Trump's Conservative
nomination Gorsuch the Supreme Court judgeship.,

As Hillary Clinton once noted during Bill's
impeachment  proceedings, "They" (The Republicans)
"go for the jugular".
They do indeed. Conservatives, convinced they alone
have cornered  the truth and righteous market, lie,
cheat, steal, violate the Rule of Law, the Constitution,
and murder those who oppose them, to install the
Conservative gospel across the land.

The point being that when I watched America's
pulse grow fainter and flatter on the monitor with every
hour of Trump's presidency, and no doctors in the
room,  I began to realize (1) Conservative Republicans
– there were none who were not Conservative after
Trump drove Senator Flake from the temple --were too
gutless, too, corrupt, and too sold out to the
Conservative Republican Party to confront, or even
disagree with Trump, much less clip his talons. (2)
Trump controlled the Executive, Judicial, and
Legislative  branches of Government. (3) Trump hired
Attorney General Barr and therefore controlled the
Department of Justice responsible for interpreting the
Mueller Report in a light favorable to Trump and
creating DOJ policywhich allowed Trump to be above
the law, to wit, President Trump could not be found
guilty of crimes he committed as long as he was a
sitting President.(4)Trump controlled  the national, print
media, state, and local TV news, and social media with
his outrageous, pejorative , threatening and bullying
tweets, and by his daily forays into events solely to get
him front page attention, and the good, benefit, or harm

to the Country and its citizens be damned!(5) Trump controlled the military as its Commander-in-Chief, even though Poppy Trump bought off a New York podiatrist to find a bone spur on his son's foot so Trump could escape serving his country in the Vietnam. War – Trumpwith his Mussolini bullfrog facial expression, saber-rattling, strutting bravado, (6) Trump mauled the media with his propaganda blitzkrieg to malign immigrants from Central and South America in order to create a scapegoated hate group just as Hitler did the Jews, (Bullying is what Narcissistic Personality Disorders must do to reassert their delusion of superiority). (7) Trump dominated the international*Zeitgeist* by threatening war with North Korea, Syria, Venezuela,, and Iran. declared a trade war with  China, and Mexico, reneged on the Trans-Pacific Partnership,, DACA, the Paris Agreement, and the Iran Nuclear Deal, yet sucking up to Putin, while thumbing his nose at his own intelligence agencies, amid mocking the incontrovertible evidence that Putin had aided and abetted Trump's counterfeit election in 2016. (Deluded Trump never could accept the reality that he still lost the popular vote to Clintonby three million votes.)  (8) Trump controlled 35-42 percent of the Americans polled no matter how many lies, he told them, (100,000 and counting), how much he seduced them with promises not his to make – US Presidents don't build walls, don't make foreign presidents pay for walls, don't void acts passed by  Congress (Affordable Care Act), and don't create jobs. Companies and businesses do.  (As I mentioned in one of the books the Prosecutor was waving in the air, all contracts  obtained by fraud, are vitiated – declared null and void, as if the contract never existed.  Therefore, Trump, having been elected by fraudulent misrepresentation, his presidency should have been voided, Trump removed, andClintonThat said, Trump's "troops," as so called in my other book, like Hitler's brown shirts present a clear and present danger as cannon fodder for Trump's *coup d'état* – Trump has already hinted he will not "go kindly into that good night," may or may not accept the election results, suggesting  he may pull a Putin, and anoint himself eternal Emperor of the Unholy American Empire.

The question each of you must ask of yourself: "Knowing now that which  the majority of Americans knew, would not you,  as an American patriot, after waiting nearly four years, for someone or some group to save the Republic, reluctantly and with heavy heart, have stepped forward even if so doing  would probably result in being sentenced to die by the very people  you thought to save?

## Day Three

Judge Vance to Prosecutor Brody: "You may call your first witness."

Brody; "I call Richard Otis,, to the stand."

Judge Vance; "As you have chosen to represent yourself, I am dissuaded to offer you advise or counsel. However, in greater service to the Constitution and the cause of Justice, I am counseled to remind you that the Fifth Amendment of the Bill of Rights, in pertinent part states, "nor shall you be compelled, in any criminal case to be a witness against yourself – you have a Fifth Amendment right to remain silent."

Dr. Otis: "I appreciate you straying from the formidable boundaries of Judicial protocol on my behalf. It seems that in your case, I erred in my assessment of you as Bush II's choices of judges. I apologize.

That said, I believe I can best launder the truth in the sunlight of open battle with the Prosecutor than would be obtained in the suspicion of guilt accruing, however innocently, from my silence or Fifth Amendment's protections."

Judge Vance: "You will be treading where the angels fear to tread.."

Dr. Otis: "I fear these matters, would intimidate the bravest of angels."

Judge Vance: "What then of jurors?"

Dr. Otis: "Their mortal existence grants  them consideration over the immortal fiction of angels."

Bailiff: "You swear to tell the truth, the whole truth, and nothing but the truth, so help you, God?"

Dr. Otis: "I will tell the truth, but not the whole truth, as I have little chance in knowing more than Plato' s shadow of the truth.

The first truth being that there is no God, thus, I would be lying if I swore to tell the truth, the whole truth, and nothing but the truth to a God which didn't exist "

Brody: Your Name?"

Dr. Otis: "Richard Otis.

Brody: "Your real name?

Dr. Otis: " Dr. Richard Otis, IV

Brody: "Your legal name?"

Dr. Otis: "Dr. Richard Granville Otis, IV.

Brody: "I warn you, this Court prosecutes perjury. According to this Certified copy of your Birth Certificate your name is Richard Coleman Granville  Jr.

Dr. Otis: My father was adopted by  Granvilles – Jeanette and Augustus Perry Granville."

Brody; "I know, but that makes you Richard Coleman Granville, not Richard Granville Otis."

Dr. Otis: "My father died in 1987, or 1988. I was working with an autistic four-year old boy, in Marion, North Carolina whose medical doctor father from India stated he would fire me If I went to the funeral."

Brody: "You did not attend your father's funeral?"

Dr. Otis: "Under those conditions, I could not."

Brody: "You can't even remember the year your father died?"

Dr. Otis: " 1987 or 8 – nearly 30 years ago. … While going through a box of my father's memorabilia ten years later still, which my half-brother released after determining the contents were of no value to him, I came across an index card -sized copy of my father's real Birth Certificate which listed his parents as Richard Otis II and his mother as Inez Mary Otis.

In deference to my real lineage, I subsequently changed my name from Granville to Otis."

Brody: "So, you can neither attest to the year of your father death, nor attending your father's funeral, leading this  Court to conclude, your relationship with your father was less than it should have been?"

Dr. Otis: "Less than it might have been."

Brody: "A source who knew, said you and your father had stopped speaking for 20 years and that your father had forbidden family members to mention your name."

Dr. Otis: "I couldn't have known that could I."

Brody: "Wouldn't have known you and your father went 20 years without speaking?"

Dr. Otis: "Couldn't have known he had forbidden my sister, brother, and half-brother to mention my name?"

Brody: "You hadn't spoken to your sister or brother for 20 years?"

Dr. Otis: "My father threw me out when I was 15. I went back to live with his adoptive parents --- my adoptive grandparents in Massachusetts."

Brody: "What did you do that was so bad as to get your father to throw you out of his house? We couldn't find a juvenile criminal record,"

Dr. Otis: "I bought a used bike with a motor attached – this would have been 1951 – for $60, I had earned that summer picking beans for two cents a pound, strawberries for four cents a box and hoeing corn for 25 cents an hour – never making more than $14 dollars a week – 8-5 – Monday---Friday –30-35 cents an hour."                                    Dr. Otis: "He got all red-faced  because I had spent $60 and done so without his permission so he reasoned I must be evicted."

Brody: "Why didn't you say so from the beginning? Do you always tell only that part of the story which generates a favorable response? Is that what we must expect from all future testimony?"

Dr. Otis: "Your rush to judgment commits the same affront to the truth of which you accuse me. The rest of the story is that by 1951, my father had becomeconsumed with bitterness from having been rejected by his biological mother at birth, abandoned in an orphanage until age two, never bonding with his adoptive father, who was off fighting Germans in the trenches of France in World War I, rejected by his judgmental and disappointed adoptive mother absorbed in preempting sin just before its inevitable seduction, who never smiled lest she become vulnerable to sin's ambush … My mother's German, Harvard graduated, father who three times denied, my father permission to marry my teen-age mother, herself the victim of tormented parents, (my biological grandparents ) whose adultery was resolved by fraudulently claiming my mother was her mother's sister, not her daughter ..

Walking home from kindergarten at age four, I discerned a sailor in my mother's bed, who she claimed was "sick and I'm taking care of him."

I knew my mother was lying. I was only four, but I knew. (My father had gone to Hartford to find work for an insurance company).

My father never recovered from the divorce  – on his dying bed at age 74,, he sobbed like an infant claiming the divorce was due to the meddling of his adoptive mother and her biological daughter, several years my father's senior, who in turn, scorned my father and his three children as being second class members of her family.

… I was sent to one foster home and my sister and brother to another, not to be reunited  until six years later when my father remarried, and who, without talking to me, tricked me into visiting him and his new wife on Labor Day in 1946. But when I readied to get into the car to with my adoptive grandparents, they told me I had to stay with my father – It had already been planned, but no one had thought to tell me or ask me what I wanted– my own father was kidnapping me – forcing me to vacate the only home – the only security, the only sense of family – of belonging  - 1 would ever know.-- leave my friends who admired me for kicking the kickball over the roof of the school, scoring the most touchdowns in recess games of "Russian Schmuck" being elected the fifth-grade King of The May …

I never forgave him.

Brody: "You have hated your father ever since."

Dr. Otis: "It was as if I never went to school for the next four years – been raised – schooled by wolves! The old two-story, white, wooden, school house was the only school – grades1-6, downstairs; grade7-12 upstairs. Each teacher taught two grades in the same room --lecture one side of the room while the other side did busy work -- at best, a 50% education. One senior class graduated only five students.

I remember learning nothing for four years. The boys were going to work their father's farm or work in a factory in Nashua, making school irrelevant, but compulsory, so classroom discipline was like being in a prison yard."

Brody: "You know about prison yards how?"

Dr. Otis; "The farm boys' major classroom activity in Miss Greenleaf's 7th grade, was picking up one's dropped pencil, in order to look up her dress,  I learned so little in grades 6-9, that –after my father threw me out and I went back to live with my adoptive grandparents, for grades 10-12, --I had to repeat French I, algebra I, and got my only "D" ever in 10th grade

English Grammar. I never did make up for those four lost years academically until my sophomore year in college, when I finally taught myself to be a student. And of course, I had also lost four years of football, baseball, hockey, and basketball. Ok, I had been on the starting high school basketball and baseball teams as a 7th grader, but that had more to do with the lack of native talent, than my ability, proven by the fact that I was cut from the basketball team when I transferred ...Even so, I was only one of two sophomores who started on the varsity football team, but I never did catch up with baseball and hockey, although I was  co-captain of the baseball team my senior year.

The high school hockey team won the State championship my senior year, but there was no hockey team for me to play on grades 6-9, so I was left out of the fun of playing on a state championship, thanks to my father.

To make matters worse, I was now attending the same high school as my father -- the principal and all my teachers had taught my father.

I only hoped they didn't connect me to him, but I could tell by the look on Principal Pollard's face when he registered me that he made the connection. (I assumed my father had done no better in high school than he had in later life.)

Brody: "Was there ever a time when you didn't hate your father?"

Dr. Otis: "-- He became disabled by multiple sclerosis, within months after I arrived that Labor Day to begin the sixth grade."

Brody: "You hated him for that too?'

Dr. Otis: "It was the cumulative effect of my father's now renewed decent into the living hell into which he now dragged the rest of the family -- his new wife, her PTSD  brother who seemed never to have recovered from his part in the assault on the beaches of Anzio, Italy, my six months-old half – actually, by size, my one/fourth baby brother, my sister, age 8 and brother, age 6, with whom I had not lived in six years, making us three strange estranged siblings, in a strained and strange land, so as night follows day, every three days, my father's rants and curses about his new wife's shell-shocked brother living upstairs, while running his father's once prosperous dairy and apple orchard, into decay – wormy inedible apples on unpruned skeletal trees, ten old cows, a few chickens and fewer geese, the 20 year-old farm horse, called "Lady" but who now gave no reason for such a lofty title. And, there's the rub – I couldn't forgive my father for his scapegoating of step-uncle Albert: His chickens and their eggs and milk from those old cows fed us and provided my ersatz uncle with the only source of family income that first year – my father in wheel chair and my mother on maternity leave from teaching home Ec – I was stealing almond chocolate candy bars from the only store in town because I was always hungry.

Brody: "So you do have a juvenile criminal record after all."

Dr. Otis: "-- So about every three days my father's cursing his fate, and/ or excoriating his wife's brother, AND needing a scapegoat, who, in truth, did smell like the rear of a cow's stall in early morning, and who sometimes seemed more like his cows than us – the rumor he romanced his cows or sheep, found no place at the table of a pre-pubescent/late blooming city boy.

In truth, I found no reason to be interested in birds and bees and with no father to explain  the relevance – my marriage bed being a too untimelya place for birds and bees to be explained.

There were to be no conversations between father and son about birds and bees or anything else, as "not talking" was my father's coping strategy of choice , so father and son would not talk to each other from 1951, until 1997 ..."

Brody; "Forty-six years is a lot of hate!"

Dr. Otis: "There was one – not a conversation, but an ultimatum implied, but not stated. Beginning when I was four – I was never to mention my mother's name, or ask any questions about her, like why she never called, or sent me a birthday or Christmas card.

Anyway, every three days, my father would say something to make my step-mom cry. It fell upon my shoulders, literally, age 10-15, to hold my step-mom, and counsel her until she stopped crying, only to repeat the ritual three days later.'

I hated my father for mistreating my step-mother. She had done nothing to deserve his bitterness, cussing, and displaced rage."

Brody: "You admit hating your father since you were a kid."

Dr. Otis:        "-- Calling my step-mother "plain" may be the most charitable description of her pulchritude, but she was a good, honest, hardworking, self-sufficient, frugal, old school,  New Hampshire, Yankee, as opposed to a Massachusetts Yankee, who she resented ... it may have been more a Protestant

versus Catholic thing – In any event, she bore the cross
of my father's crippled psyche and his equally crippled
three – soon two -- offspring, in order to have a child,
who she showered with every indulgence allowed
according to her circumstance as a home ec teacher,
supporting an invalid husband, and my sister and
brother, who enjoyed no such indulgence, nor should,
or could,  they have,

Brody; "And all this has to do with you
assassinating the President of the United States how?"

Dr. Otis: "In defense of my Country against a
ruthless and mentally deranged Dictator --"

Brody: "Assassination."

Dr. Otis: "As his first born, the ghosts of his
failures – gas station jobs during the Depression – The
best he could do was fix music boxes for the Boston
Music Company, bad marriages, his seemingly cursed
loser mentality– his head in photos was always down,
his pervasive unhappiness – that same look of
Lincolnesque sadness from a life of accrued rejection
and dead dreams. Most tormenting of the ghosts
invading my unguarded thoughts, my father's multiple
sclerosis takes top billing,though the other ghosts,
usurping center  stage without provocation. haunt me as
if his fate must be my future ...I pitied him, I wept in
private over each of his slings and arrows of such
outrageous misfortune, but I could not love him, lest in
loving him I might be tempted to join – share his frailty
as if it were mine as self-fulfilling prophecy.-- the
respect that makes calamity of such a long life.

In truth I may have subconsciously provoked
him to banish me, predicting my adoptive grand-parents

would take me back, not considering that my father would literally cast me out with no place  to go."

But, in retrospect, it wasn't just what he did – put me in a foster home  separated from my sister and brother– instead of providing safety as Freud cites is the first order of  business for all fathers – made me afraid I might be there for the rest of my life … never visited me – never  told me what I had done so bad as to be sent to live away from my family to a strange place  -- banished at age four to live with a man I'd never seen before, who didn't like me and I didn't like him.

He tried to enroll me in a school nearby, but I was too young so he was stuck with me all day …

My father did pick me up one time – it may have been Thanksgiving or Christmas ...to take me to his adoptive parents for dinner ...I'm riding next to him in the front seat it's 1940, because I was four – Suddenly, my father begins sobbing uncontrollably, I hug his neck, saying "It's going to be OK."

The two lane road turns 90 degrees – we're heading for a telephone pole – I see it as if I'm there – I grab the steering wheel and jerk it to the left causing us to bump up on the sidewalk but missing the telephone pole … Reflecting on that incident as an adult. I believe my father intended to kill us both...

It seemed like forever, but was probably less than a year – my adoptive grandmother convinced a Norfolk County Judge to change my status from being a ward of the State of Massachusetts to living with her. I don't believe my father allowed her to be awarded Guardianship, which would explain, how he managed to take me live with him when I was 10, after he married my step- mom...

My father must have gone back to live with his adoptive parents after the divorce and after we were placed in foster homes, because he was there, when I arrived, and lived there until he married my step-mom five years later.

Though my father lived there, he was more like my uncle, than my father. His adoptive mother – my adoptive grandmother was captain of the ship, and the three male seamen– my adoptive grandfather my father, and I were her deckhands.

It was from an ancient grudge that my father and his adoptive parents, reunited. First my father and his adoptive father were aliens in a strange land. His adoptive father was fighting Germans in the trenches of France when my father was a wee lad of 5 and six, the time of bonding having passed. Besides, his adoptive father, had already bonded with his biological daughter, several years older than my father, and was never enthusiastic, about adopting a second child.

The only time the three makeshift generations did something together was attending a Red Sox  game at Fenway Park. We sat along the third base line. Joe Cronin was the Red Sox shortstop, The year was either 1943,or 1944.

In any event he and my father never bonded, nor did they seem to even like each other – one a 240 pound, gourmand who never tasted a food he didn't like,  a former army major as member of the Yankee Division, who joined the army at age 16, fought in the Spanish- American War and World War I, a wood-carver, Civil War buff, who made a pilgrimage  in 1937 from Needham, Massachusetts to Gettysburg, PA, where he walked the battlefield in Lee's boots – war was not death, amputations, and field's of corpses, but rather a sanitized saccharin  chess match between opposing generals. (The largest painting in his Yankee home was of Confederate officer Robert Jocelyn, for whom he named his second granddaughter.)

For his part, his adopted son – my father- was a skinny kid of 135 pounds, who was rejected by the Army for "flat feet" having lost three fingers in factory accident and being the father of three children, born in 1936, 1938, and 1940, who became a Lincolnphile, and whose ambition was to become a professional singer like his idols Enrico Caruso and Bing Crosby..

As to my father's adoptive mother, she seems never to have forgiven him for his teen-age obsession to find his biological parents-- the Boston Brahmin Otises.

By the time, my father and I were living with his adoptive mother – my adoptive grandmother – the resentment between ersatz mother and son, had become the proverbial elephant in the room,

Had she rescued me from the foster home, because she cared about me, or to get back at my father for his betrayal? The evidence suggests the latter, for she did  in fact usurp the role of my mother – in  his eyes spoiling me –  raising me better than she had raised my father, adding to his bitterness and his resentment of me.

Three generations of  loveless, resentful, openly hostile, quasi-family relationships ...I never witnessed affection between my adoptive grandparents, between them and my father, between my father and mother, nor my father and me -- cold, distant, judgmental Episcopalian New Englanders. ...

Neither my mother nor my father ever told me they loved mebecause -- because they didn't – couldn't -- Their parents never loved them. My mother's parents claimed she wasn't theirs, but was her mother's sister, and my father spent his first two years in an orphanage."

Brody; "And for that you hated your father – hated him so much you assassinated President Trump – You couldn't get back at your father because he was dead."

Dr. Otis: "Objection, Judge. Not a question, but a conclusory statement appropriate only during the Prosecution's summation."

Judge Vance: "Sustained."

Dr. Otis: "I didn't hate my father until years later...the cumulative effect of putting me in foster home without warning or explanation,  never talking to me about my mother -- where she was, why she left, was she ever coming back, what I had done to be rejected by her, talk to me about stuff a young boy needed to hear from his father.

Instead, he either cussed like truck driver when frustrated, but went silent about personal issues – like throwing me out of the house and not speaking to me for 40 years while ordering my sister and brother to never mention my name.

Why didn't he visit me at the foster home? I was only four years old! I was scared to appear scared! He picked me up once, but would have killed us both if I hadn't  jerked the steering wheel to keep us from crashing into that telephone pole at 35 miles per hour...Looking back, it felt like I was the adult and he was the child...

He tricked me into visiting him. When I  got
ready to go back home with my adoptive grandparents,
my adoptive grandmother announced I was staying with
my father – no warning, no discussion, no one asking
me what I wanted to do.

Did my father try to console me. No, not once.
In fact, he ignored me. He had finally stood up to his
deeply resented – perhaps truly hated, adoptive mother,
who had raised  me as the son he had never been…

My father and my adoptive  grandmother, each by
their own selfish malicious ways, used me to avenge
their life-long grudges against the other, all the while
pretending each gave a damn about me – passing me
back and forth demanding my allegiance to shame the
other. Yet, at no time did either one say the words to me
I so longed to hear, but never did -- "I love you." –

Judge Vance: to Dr. Otis: "Do you need a
recess? "

Dr. Otis: "Sorry. I-- I – Eighty years, and still
grief's energy has lost nothing to time's regulation ...
My father *de facto* had detained me, a minor child,
against my will, with the intention to cause me harm,
and did cause me great harm.He kidnapped me!"

Brody: "Like you kidnapped your daughter ?"

Dr. Otis: "I call for a mistrial! The Prosecutor
has entered information of alleged past acts, the
Prosecutor knows to be inadmissible"

Brody: "Withdrawn."

Dr. Otis: "The horse has already bolted  out of
the barn."

Judge Vance: "Motion for a mistrial is denied."

Dr. Otis: "Exception. I will appeal.

Judge Vance: That is your right."

Brody: "What was this  "great harm" you claim your father caused you/"

Dr. Otis: " –My father who, as Freud counseled, was supposed to keep his child safe, tricked me – I was only ten – into going for a visit on Labor Day, knowing he was going to make me stay with him, when my home – the only home I would ever have –with the only parents I would ever know – the only sense of belonging, however tenuous, I would ever feel, was with my adoptive grandparents.

I was a misfit from that Labor Day in 1946, until my father banished me four years later.

Soon after I arrived, my step-mother-- more the spectator than co-conspirator, her lesbian younger sister/army nurse and her "shell-shocked younger brother, put me on a horse facing backward, took my picture as the "city kid" from Massachusetts who didn't know the head from the horse's ass, and would, from time to time, present the picture as entertainment at family gatherings.

My six grade teacher, Miss Deneau French Canadian  – a mean, sadistic, divorcee, who hated kids, but nonetheless, favored the one or  two  rich kids, one day ordered me to sweep the classroom floor, and then jeeringly called me out, "What's the matter city boy; no one ever taught you how to sweep a floor?"

Another time, upon coming in from recess, one of rich kids complained that I had cheated by claiming I was safe at third base because David had dropped the ball instead of tagging me, to which Miss Deneau maliciously scolded me, "Nobody likes a cheater."

The next house down the road about a quarter of a mile toward Nashua, lived Bobby Nartoff, an 18 years old senior, who took a special interest in sixth grade,10 year old me, and, when walking the nearly the two miles home from school, would ask me to continue pass my house and down the wooded road out of sight, where he would hug and kiss me for several minutes.

I knew nothing about homosexuality, "faggots," "queers" or sexual molestation, of which there was none.

My father should have asked me questions if he gave a damn about what happened to me, but he didn't. He'd gotten me away from my adoptive grandmother – his adoptive mother --getting even with both of us at the same time.

' … In high school, I was molested by my senior English teacher who, to get me out of town, persuaded me to hop a train to Greensboro, North Carolina, where one of his former students had married a psychology professor, who assured him he would get me into Duke or somewhere ..

Also during my senior year in high school, our family doctor, who was making house calls to my adoptive dying grandfather, while giving me a physical exam for football in his office, removed all his clothes except his jockey shorts, hopped up on the treatment table, announcing, "I can get you into Harvard Medical School, but first you'll have to learn how to give a massage."

"Mr. Brody, if you are trying to show motive, to wit, that my hatred of my father was the direct and proximate cause of my interdicting Trump's treasonous and criminal destruction of America's Constitutional Republic, I would be obstructing justice – withholding evidence -- if I omitted the following: (We are, after all first and foremost, pursuing justice, not winning this case – Better to lose if justice prevails, than to win an unjust verdict, n'est pas?

That summer between 7[tth] and 8th grades -  the summer of 1948  – I remember Babe Ruth died on August 16 -- I worked on my step-mother's Uncle George's dairy farm. (He must have been in his 70's. He always walked/limped with a cane.)

I was 12.

I had to get up each morning at 5:30 to ride with my step- mother's oldest brother, only next door neighbor, and a machinist working in Fitchburg, Massachusetts, 30 minutes away.

My typical workday, started at 7 AM, at which time I would fill the bin with wood for the kitchen cook stove, then clean cows stalls and haul buckets of water for the cows and pull down hay in the barn loft for them to eat, weed the large vegetable garden with a small Farmall tractor, I taught myself to drive.

Aunt Kay would fix lunch.. Once a week, the yard needed mowing with a hand pushed mower, shrubs around the house needed weeding by hand, vegetables picked -- squash, beans, melons, corn, and hay cut, dried, and then loaded by pitchfork, onto a trailer, carried to the barn, then hoisted into the loft.

I expected to be paid something, but, as with everything involving my father, pay was never mentioned.

September came and went; no word from Uncle George or my father about paying me.        Mid-October, my step-mother informs me Uncle George had mailed me a Defense Bond worth $18.75 – one dollar

and 87 cents a week, for 10 weeks, .04 cents an hour,
$.37 cents a day!

That's when I realized my father had used my
indentured labor for the whole summer of 1948 to pay
for the nine months he, my step-mother, sister and
brother had stayed with Uncle George  and Aunt Kay
while my step-mother's house was being renovated!

That had been the plan before I even moved to
New Hampshire.

At that moment I looked at the Government
bond for $18.75, I realized my father hated me –was not
my father, but my enemy who had always resented the
fact that his adoptive mother treated me better –
probably to get back at him for being such a
disappointed to her – than she had treated him."

Brody: "Which you and Oswald over came with
world-wide attention for having assassinated the
world's most powerful person – the President of the
United States."

Dr. Otis: "…My bedroom, which was no room
at all, but instead, space at the top of stairs. large
enough to accommodate an old army cot, leading to my
step-uncle's bedroom, was moved to the back unglassed
and unscreened porch on the back of the house, I was
sleeping outside – year round.        Sometimes there
would be snow on the bed when I woke up in the
morning, and I remember one winter the thermometer
on the door into the kitchen read 20 degrees below zero
three nights in a row.

… Up on the knoll behind the porch some 40
feet was an old, rusted, oil, drum, pocked with shotgun
pellets …during the worst of times

– I'd look out into the night at the shadow of the old shot up oil barrel figuring how I could put my gun on the porch railing, with string from the trigger to where I was standing in front of the oil drum so I could pull the trigger... More often I tried to will my heart to stop – waiting death's advantage over sleep's merciless dreams...'

Brody; "So, rather than turn your rage on yourself – commit suicide, you chose homicide – the murder of the President of the United States."

Dr. Otis: "Matching your irrelevant rush to judgment with my rush to end this painful visit with my past, I submit the following summary of my seasons of discontent. I never forgave my father for dumping me in a foster home without notice or explanation, killing us both, if I had not grabbed the steering wheel, moving me to New Hampshire against my will and in violation of my best interests and welfare, forcing me to live  out of reach of my role model – my idealized and credible father – Ted Williams, absent any discussion or consent making me an indentured servant to an Uncle George, for ten weeks at $1.87 a week,
removing me from one of the best school systems in Massachusetts, where he had attended K-12, and graduated, to a one, old, two-story wooden, firetrap building where each teacher taught two grades in the same classroom,  from which I learned nothing in four years --I would have fared far better had I been raised by wolves. I had to repeat most of my classes when I transferred, back to Massachusetts grade 9-12,never did catch up, thereby restricting my colleges choices already severely limited by funds. (Neither my father,

my mother, step-mother, adoptive grandmother, who had inherited the equivalent of $154,000 in 2020, from the estate of her brother in California. nor my adoptive grandfather-- paid a dime toward my 10 years of college. Neither did my Harvard graduate maternal grandfather, who refused to acknowledge that I was his first born grandchild. In fact during all the visits to his house – I even had a crib in his bedroom, I don't remember him ever speaking to me – much less holding me.(My maternal grandmother/school teacher,  sent me $20.00 my sophomore semester at Elon.)

My father never spoke to me or contacted me from the day he threw me out in 1951, until I visited him in the hospital  after he suffered his first stroke prior to when he died in 1987 or 8, making it problematic for the Court to claim an act alleged to have occurred in 2020 , was motivated by the interaction between my father and I last occurring in 1951, 70 years earlier.

Brody: "Not the Defendant's problem."

Dr. Otis: "But it wasn't just what he did, but what he failed to do as a father.-- teach me how to tie a tie, about foreskin, sex, periods,  babies – I was in high school and still ignorant as to the creation process and still  a virgin at age 21, until seduced by a college classmate in a room in the administration building on a Saturday afternoon.

There is information a son can only learn from his father, which was also a problem, albeit of far less magnitude. First, because he so deeply resented – hated me-- wanted me to fail, he was certainly not going give me any info that might be helpful. Second, my father's repertoire of communication was limited cussing to an oath of reticence. Third, he was most loquacious when cussing – yet swearing a blue steak is not the forum Polonius used to counsel Laertes: "Neither a borrower nor a lender be, listen more than you talk and this above all; to thine ownself be true, and it must follow, as the night follows the day, thou canst not then be false to any man."

All my father had to do was give me a copy of Polonius' advice  to his son – What greater gift could a father give his son?"

"…This trial, by exhuming memory's corpses, exposes errors in  the coroner's cause of death long after the statute of limitations, to wit, the true cause of the death of my relationship with my father now appears to be that the relationship never lived --was DOA. – Still-born six months before I was born – an unwanted pregnancy by which parent? Both?

My father and I were not father and son, but, in truth, sibling rivals – Cain – my dad and Abel – me, for the love and affection of his adoptive mother  and  my adoptive grandmother, whose severe  Puritanism upbringing precluded her from having any love and affection to give, or as H.L. Mencken opined, "Puritanism is the haunting fear that someone (me) somewhere (her house) might be happy."

In ten years under her roof, I never  remember her smiling – even in her pictures.

My bedroom in her house had one closet, over which a cloth curtain hung on a rod. I remember believing my grandmother was hiding behind the curtain waiting for me to fall asleep, so she could come out and kill me.) … I was the innocent child who two adults used to get back at the other.

In either case, my father was now my enemy from whom I must escape…. But how and when?

My unwitting purchase of an used motorbike for $ 60 dollars I saved from my summer earnings without consulting my father, who never talked to me about my mother or anything else, answered the questions how and when I would escape my enemy – my father.
So there you have the rest of the story, told in naked narrative absent any and all pretext as to whether it be received favorably or unfavorably

Finally, I would be remiss if I failed to sympathize with Mr. Brody's mission impossible plight of trying to find probable cause among the most improbable, irrelevant, and untimely events."

Brody: "Unfavorably. By indulging you in this boring odyssey, the Court let you hang yourself, to wit, you gave the  State motive via your belabored explanation of your hatred of your father who, like Lee Harvey Oswald's *in absentia*  hatred of his father lead to his assassination of President Kennedy, in your case lead to the assassination of President Trump.

Dr. Otis; "Motion to Strike. The State has willfully misapprehended the rules of evidence by inserting Closing Argument, where a question is proper.."

Judge Vance: "Sustained.!"

Brody: "Stephen Diamond wrote in *Psychology Today,* Oswald's father died two months before Lee was born, leaving him fatherless, feeling abandoned, impotent, angry, isolated, precluded from being or feeling manly, and therefore, in an Oedipal rage, killed, not his father, but the "father of his country' President Kennedy."

Dr. Otis: "Motion to Strike as Closing Argument, not a proper question".

Judge Vance: "Sustained."

Brody: You have told this Court, at great length, how you hated your father, citing in detail the reasons for your hatred, is that correct?"

Dr. Otis: "As I recalled those incidents –were limited to events from the time I was four years old until I was 15, when he ordered me to leave.– some 70 – 80 years ago."

Brody: "The Court is impressed with the accuracy of those details. How many years was it that you did not speak to, or communicate with your father?"

Dr. Otis: "!1951- 1986?'"

Brody: " 35years?"

Dr. Otis; "I don't know exactly?"

Brody; "But you do remember grabbing the steering wheel to keep your father's  car from hitting the telephone pole, when you were only --"

Dr. Otis: "Four"

Brody: "Four, but you can't – or won't – tell us how long you went without having any communication with your father."

Dr. Otis: "1951-1980-something…He died in 1987 or 8, had a stroke before that – at least 30 years."

Brody: "Not 20 as you  stated previously."

Dr. Otis: "Granted, if the State will also grant that the memory of an 84 year-old works more reliably in recounting events of 70 years ago than those of yesterday"

Brody: "But certainly a son would remember when his father died, no matter how much he hated his father."

Dr. Otis: "The State, in its rush to judgment inserts its own conclusory opinions instead of properly asking questions of the Defendant."

Brody: "Did you attend your father's funeral?"

Dr. Otis: "I have twice answered, No."

Brody; "To avoid any confusion, did you attend your father's funeral."

Dr. Otis: "I was working with a young autistic child in Marion, NC. His MD father said, if I went to my father's funeral in New Hampshire he would fire me. No I did not attend my father's funeral, and would probably not have attended anyway'"

Brody; "You hated your father that much?"

Dr. Otis: "Funerals are for the living, too lately offered the dead."

Brody: "You don't believe in an after-life?"

Dr. Otis: "Oh but I do: After life, death, during which the body immediately decomposes – changes into the worst smelling, most repugnant  gases imaginable – then dust to dust – to the earth from which it originated – in truth, an ocean. Death, due to its inexorable finality, vitiates memory. The after-life promised by various religions is the perfect biggest of big lies – Heaven being that 'undiscovered country 'whose bourne no travelers return-- puzzles the will – fear of death makes cowards of us all."

Brody: "You're an atheist."

Dr. Otis; "A non-theist, who by any name would give the same cause for a mistrial having prejudiced the jury in the most egregious way – no other label could poison the jury as well!"

Brody:"You held a grudge against your father for 40 years – so much hate to forego your father's funeral/"

Dr. Otis. " Wrong on all counts. I was not the same person who he ordered onto the streets at age 15. Over the next 30 years, mellowed by years in which I repeated his mistakes, to wit, marrying too young for the same wrong reasons – to retaliate against the parent of the young bride, haunted by the same insecurity and lack of confidence inherent in our mother's mutual rejection – my father given up for adoption at birth – my mother abandoning me at a foster home at age four, both raised by the same cold, critical, loveless, judgmental Puritanical mother surrogate – pity, sorrow., and wariness that I seemed destined for a similar fate as my father, replaced hate's former dominion, I could not attend  his funeral with such an admixture of confusion, pity, sadness, guilt, -- fear that I was so like him I must suffer the same slings and arrows of outrageous misfortune -- failure, and futility."

Brody: "People's One and Two, Your Honor. "Do you recognize these two books?'

Dr. Otis: "I do."

Brody; "Please read the title of People's Exhibit One.

Dr. Otis: "Trumps' Troops Revolt Against Republican Party's Betrayal."

Brody; "Did you write this book?"

Dr. Otis: "I did."

Brody; "Please read the highlighted portions on the last two pages.."

Dr. Otis: "Their ploy unraveled in 2015, when the 90% who identified themselves
as Republicans concluded the Republican Party had betrayed them – taken their votes and run – offered them no protection against "Dubya's Depression," no bailout to save their homes from foreclosure, denied them Obamacare just to spite the Democratic President, no protection against US companies moving jobs overseas – threw them under the bus as so much collateral damage in their war to defeat that "uppity nigger.

Every dog has its day." The 90% Republicans would avenge their betrayal by the Republican Party by becoming troops in Mr. Trump's battle with the Republican Party insiders – like Jeb Bush, and Rubio and false prophets like Ted Cruz,"

Brody: "Is it fair to say that from the beginning, you had it in for President Trump – were out to get him at any cost?"

Dr. Otis; "No. It is fair to say, that I wrote that Trump exploited the working class due to Republican insider President Bush
II's Depression, by fraudulently claiming they had lost their homes and jobs due to President Obama's policies and programs.

It was lie. Trump knew it was a lie told to get elected in 2016."

Brody: "Lies were told by both sides,"

Dr. Otis: "Oh, you mean like Trump --"

Brody; "President Trump --"

Dr. Otis: "Trump claiming there were "fine people on both sides" in Charlottesville, VA in 2017 – both sides meaning the violent white supremacists,

Neo-Fascists brandishing military assault rifles to prevent the other side –unarmed protesters from demanding the  statute of Robert Lee, general of evil Confederacy, based on slavery, be removed..”

Brody: “People's Exhibit Two. “Why and How We the People Must Remove Trump.” Did you write this book?”

Dr. Otis: “Yes.”

Brody: “Please read he highlighted portion at the bottom of page 66.”

Dr. Otis: “Trump's Narcissistic Personality Disorder renders him unable to fulfill his contract as President of the United  States.”

Brody: “And what contract is that?”

Dr. Otis; “His employment contract: “I do solemnly swear (or affirm) that I will faithfully execute the Office of the President of the United States, and will, to the best of my ability, preserve, protect, and defend the Constitution of the United States.” for four years at a salary of $400. That contract. In truth, Trump had no ability -- was untrained with no experience, and a mental disorder rendering the governance of the public impossible. Trump abused, altered, and betrayedthe Constitution in bad faith for four years at a salary he neither deserved nor needed.”

Brody: “By what authority are you entitled to make the diagnosis of Narcissistic Personality Disorder?”

Dr. Otis; “I have a Ph.D. in psychology.”
Brody: “Licensed?”
Dr. Otis: “Not required in this instance.”
Brody; “But you were licensed in the past?”
Dr. Otis: “I was.”

Brody; "From when to when?"

Dr. Otis: "Objection. Irrelevant."

Judge Vance: "Overruled."

Dr. Otis: "1973-1983."

Brody:"License ever revoked, or not renewed?"

Dr. Otis: "I let it lapse."

Brody: "People's Three. It says here, your license was revoked by the North Carolina Board of Psychology Examiners for

having used testimonials in your  ads for your stop smoking clinics."

Dr. Otis: "Objection-- Irrelevant. Prior acts inadmissible as being offered for the pejorative purpose to prejudice the jury against the Defendant."

Judge Vance: "Sustained."

Brody: "People's Four.Is this a copy of an ad you placed in the Raleigh News and Observer in 1982, listing you as the owner/operator of stop smoking clinics operating under the name Dr. Granville's Stop Smoking Clinics?"

Dr. Otis; "Yes."

Brody: "As a matter of public record, did the State  of North Carolina, revoke your license to practice psychology for having used testimonials in your newspaper ads?"

Dr. Otis: "Again irrelevant and inadmissible as being offered for the pejorative purpose to prejudice the jury against the Defendant, but also made in bad faith, misleading and incorrect.

I will nevertheless set the record straight. First, having never smoked, yet naively convinced most smokers wanted to quit smoking and would quit if a program based on scientific principles were offered them, and having invested in aa program, to wit, a program conditioning the smoker to experience nausea with smoking cigarettes. Second, being a northerner, unaware of North Carolina's worship of the tobacco plant and that the sin of smoking built the Southern Baptist churches, and many of its colleges, most noteworthy being Duke University, and third, yet to experience the oxymoron "southern justice" and that Jim Crow still nested in the North Carolina's courthouses, I opened quasi-franchised stop smoking clinics in Raleigh, and later Durham and Chapel Hill.

In my half page Grand Opening ad in the *Raleigh News and Observer*, developed by a purported friend and owner of an advertising agency whose help always turned out badly for me, included testimonials of smokers from the franchiser 's program in Arkansas, for which they had signed their permission with a photo to use by all the franchisees.

Behind my back, presumably by a jealous/envious Raleigh psychologist, too much the coward to contact me first as required by Ethical Standards for Psychologists, reported me to the North Carolina Licensing Board of Practicing Psychologists, who sent me a notice alleging I had violated ethical principles of psychologists by using testimonials in my Grand Opening ad in the *Raleigh, News and Observer,* implying I was being sanctioned and my clinics closed.

I countered in a letter to the Board; (1) There is no stigma attached to smokers as there is to persons diagnosed with mental disorders. (2) Smokers in Arkansas had willingly given written permission to use their testimonials and photos. (3) None of the other 50 franchisers had encountered a problem with the testimonials in their states. (4) The ex-smokers had shared their testimonials and photos in a good faith effort to encourage other smokers to follow their example. (5) Therefore, I had not violated any ethical principles, to the contrary, the testimonials served to encourage Raleigh smokers to quit, which was obviously to their benefit.

But, the southern European-American -- the quintessential hypocrite committed to the Big Lie that slavery was not only good business, but had received the blessing of Southern Baptist god. (Lying lies in their DNA.)

The real problem with Licensing Board, whose members had been appointed by Governor Hunt, a third generation tobacco farmer from Wilson, was that I might reduce the number of smokers in Raleigh, the capitol of the nation's leading producer of tobacco.

So, the Licensing Board rushed to misapprehend my defense as a "failure to co-operate, and on that basis revoked my license without first noting I had earlier let my license lapse.

A few months later the North Carolina Attorney General announced he was shutting down my stop smoking clinics for failing to be licensed as "Entertainment"

Next the Governor's Office, "planted" two females posing as smokers wanting to quit.

It was obvious they were "plants" as they laughed, joked, and  chatted during the classes, and made no attempt to follow the directions, stated as being necessary for a refund, the request for which I rejected,

A few days later the complicit *Raleigh News and Observer*– co-conspirator – ran a story interviewing the two "plants," maligning me for reneging on my guarantee to make a full refund, fraudulentlyand maliciously omitting that part of the guarantee which states the client must follow the directions as described in their workbook, and must intend to quit smoking.

Of course, in the southern tradition of "managed news,' – highest rates of FOXNEWS watchers – the *News and Observer* never sought my side of the story, thereby earning the title "co-conspirator."

Brody; "Poor Dr. Otis – so smart, but not so smart as to avoid being the eternal victim. Were you a licensed psychologist at the time you diagnosed President Trump as a Narcissistic Personality?"

Dr. Otis: "No." I was retired, no longer a practicing psychologist, and having no need to be licensed. I could have been a professor of psychology with 30 years of teaching experience, which requires no license." but able to diagnose Trump as a Narcissistic Disorder."

Brody: "But weren't you acting illegally as a defrocked psychologist when you diagnosed President Trump?

Dr. Otis:"The arbiters as to my conclusion that Trump is – was a Narcissistic Personality Disorder is the consensus of the community of psychologists – to date I have received not one rebuttal."

Brody: "Are you familiar with the Goldwater Rule?

Dr. Otis; "I am."

Brody; Then you must know that the American Psychiatric Association and the American Psychological Association prohibit public diagnoses of persons they have not examined in an office for a required minimum of number of hours, stating. "It is unethical for psychiatrists to give a professional opinion about public figures who they have not examined in person and from whom they have not obtained consent to discuss their findings. Did you personally examine President Trump?"

Dr. Otis:"No and the American Psychological Association stated no such prohibition."

Brody; "Did you offer a professional opinion as to President Trump's mental status."

Dr. Otis: "I did."

Brody: "How often did you violate
the ethical standards of the American Psychiatric Association."

Dr. Otis; "Never."

Brody: "Never'"

Dr. Otis: "I was not a member of the American Psychiatric Association, and therefore not liable for their rules and regulations.

In 1972, Ralph Ginsburg, then editor of *Fact Magazine,* sent questionnaires to some 12,000 psychiatrists asking then
to offer their opinion as to presidential candidate Barry Goldwater's fitness for the job  of President of the United States. The consensus, published in Fact Magazine was a resounding, "Unfit, "with added comments raging from the plausible to the absurd, unwittingly exposing the unreliability of psychiatric diagnoses in general.

Admitted extremist Conservative Republican Goldwater was irate. He sued Editor Ginzburg and *Fact Magazine,* and was awarded $1.00 (one dollar) against Ginzburg, $25,000 in punitive damages against Ginzburg  and $50,000 against *Fact Magazine.*

The Conservative American Medical Association, AMA, landlord of the less Conservative American Psychiatric Association, being supporters of Goldwater were also irate – so these upstart liberal psychiatrists must be paddled – forced to draft and service the 1973 Goldwater Rule. Fast forward 43 years to Trump."

Brody: "President Trump        --"

Dr. Otis: "-- the wimpy chastised psychiatrists and more wimpy still – psychologists, scamper to hide behind the out-dated, arcane, and now irrelevant Goldwater Rule, so to avoid their duty to inform the American public of the clear and compelling evidence of the inevitable danger to the United States –its people and its Constitutional Republic caused by a Trump presidency."

Brody: "According to one over-the hill, octogenarian, defrocked psychologist with no professional standing or credibility.'"

Dr. Otis: "Is there a question?"

Brody: "Two questions: When did you examine President Trump and where is his permission to release your findings."

Dr. Otis: "My examinations of Trump--"

Brody;"President Trump-"

Dr. Otis: " – took place 2015- 2020, in Trump's natural environment, which as  Dr. Jane Goodall demonstrated, is much more reliable and realistic than that offered by a sterile, artificial, staged setting of a cage, or in the case at bar, an office, --"

Brody: "Are you denigrating – equating --the President of the United States Donald J. Trump with chimpanzees?"

Dr. Otis: "There is no research to demonstrate that Chimpanzees, lie."

Judge Vance; "Sarcasm has no place in my courtroom."

Dr. Otis: " – over an estimated 1,000 hours – Again more reliable and valid than the one-two hour psychiatric examinations I personally, observed during my internships – noting, for example, how Trump holds his nose up and arrogantly purses his lips exactly as Mussolini did, to noting how everything -- literally everything Trump says or does, is predictable from one of the nine symptoms of a Narcissistic Personality Disorder as listed in the Diagnostic and Statistical Manual of Mental Disorders DSM-5)"

Brody: "And you have a copy of President Trump's written permission to make your findings public.?'

Dr. Otis; "Irrelevant. Having made his statements and committed his actions in public – having actively commanded the public's attention, Trump has no right to a "privacy' claim.

Dr. Glass, psychiatrist at the Harvard Medical School stated, "In the case of Trump "

Brody: "President Trump--"

Dr. Otis: " In the case of Trump there is an extraordinary abundance of speech and  behavior on which one may form a judgment" as to Trump's mental status. Dr. Brandy Lee. a Yale affiliated, forensic psychiatrist, and author of October 2017 book, *The Dangerous Case of Donald Trump,* stated, Trump's mental disorder is so severe and the risks accompanying the power of the presidency so great that she had the overriding duty to warn the public. (I made many similar warnings in my tweets.)

During Trump's Impeachment in December 2019, Dr. Lee, along with 350 mental health professionals, signed a letter notifying the Impeachment tribunal that Trump's mental health was declining, thereby posing a real potential to become a more dangerous threat to the safety of the nation. which I also noted in my tweets,

Finally, in *Tarasoff v. Regents of the University of California* (1974,, 1976), the California Supreme Court ruled, "We cannot tolerate exposure to damage from concealed knowledge of the therapist that his patient was lethal."

Brody: "Irrelevant. You were not President Trump's therapist."

Dr. Otis. "But I was the person in the theater who, upon seeing Trump in the corner holding his cigarette lighter to newspaper, hurried to warn the manager."

Brody: "In your "Must Remove Trump Book," you claim that because President Trump made campaign promises he *ipso facto* had a contract with the American people, which, according to you, was fraudulently obtained, therefore voiding the contract, meaning Hillary Clinton should become president – It was a joke, right? – a bad joke trivializing President's Trump's election, and demeaning his presidency?'"

Dr. Otis: "No. It is your willful and malicious misapprehension of the book's
lawful and competent message that trivializes its legitimate thesis and this  Court's characterization of it and its author.

My claim  is simply that Trump fraudulently promised American voters he would perform acts he knew, or should have known, were not within his authority, jurisdiction,  or Constitutional right,

Some of Trump's 50 fraudulent, deceptive, abuses of presidential power and authority include: "I will appeal and replace Obamacare." (No you won't. Only Congress makes laws – and  by acting out of envy of President Obama, the welfare of Americans be damned, Trump acts contrary to his oath of office."

Judge Vance: "There will be no bad language in my Courtroom."

Dr. Otis: "The people's courtroom, for whom you labor."

Judge Vance: "When you're addressing my court, you will speak so that I can hear you!"

Dr. Otis: "-- I will build a wall at the Mexican border and make Mexico pay for it."
(Symptom #!- Narcissistic Personality-- "a grandiose sense of self-importance, exaggerates achievements and talents  expects to be recognized as being superior without commensurate achievements"

Presidents of the United States don't build walls, Congress does, and Presidents of  the United States  don't order presidents of other countries to pay for anything.)

"I'm going to be the greatest jobs president God ever made," mentioned here only because that one sentence demonstrates  the severity of Trump's mental disorder, in turn, causing every psychiatrist, psychologist, social worker, mental health worker to march on Washington demanding his candidacy be withdrawn by reason of Trump being too mentally disabled to perform the duties as President of the United States."

"I will make America great again."
"L'etatc'estmoi' – I am the State" – (Symptom #1 - Narcissistic Personality-- "a grandiose sense of self-importance, exaggerates achievements  and talents -- expects to be recognized as being superior  without commensurate achievements."

"Trump is deluded he is the second coming of Louis XIV – the Sun King – and in his rush to so anoint himself, "Trump The Greatest," overlooks this fact: He is President of the United States, despite losing the popular vote by just under three million votes to Hillary Clinton, is NOT the king of the United States – a potentially fatal miscalculation."

"I will defund Planned Parenthood because I'm pro-life," then why not fund the Southern Baptist Convention because you covet the evangelical vote?

Again, narcissistic personality Trump dangerously believes, as did Louis XIV, Napoleon Bonaparte, and Hitler, that he is the State – the United States – the government is in service of his likes and dislikes, rather than the truth – Trump is in service of the government of the United States and all Americans, a potentially fatal misapprehension on Trump's part."

"I am going to appoint judges in the mold of Scalia,"

The Constitution guarantees every American litigant a "fair and impartial " Hearing. Scalia was appointed to the US Supreme Court by extreme Conservative Poster Boy Reagan, because Scalia was also an extreme Conservative, By appointing Scalia, a known extreme Conservative Reagan violated his oath of office to protect, uphold, and defend the Constitution, guaranteeing every American citizen an impartial judiciary. By announcing he was going to "appoint judges in the mold of Scalia," Trump boasted he was going to violate this oath to support and defend the Constitution's guarantee of a fair and impartial judiciary before Trump even takes his oath. It is also relevant to note that Scalia was first about Scalia, second, the clandestine emissary for the Catholic Church, third, a devout, uncompromising Conservative Republican, and fourth ,a Supreme CourtJudge in service of the first three as exemplified in his rulings in *District of DC v. Heller* and *Citizens United* two the most flagrant assaults on the Constitutional rights of every citizen to a fair and impartial judiciary, in history.

For example in *Heller*, Scalia, *de facto* representing the NRA and white supremacists, Neo-Nazi, and vagrant vigilantes, willfully, and fraudulently re-wrote the Second Amendment to give individuals the right to bear arms individually, in self-defense, unconnected with service in a militia, when Scalia knew, or being self-proclaimed all-knowing, should have known, the Second Amendment, stipulates the Second Amendment only applies to a 'well-regulated militia.'

The Conservatives' knee-jerk attacks on liberal jurists as being "activist judges" in civil rights cases, in

*Heller,* turn themselves into over-activist judges by arbitrarily re-writing the Second Amendment to accommodate their Conservative bias, to wit, deleting the first 13 words of the Second Amendment, and then tacking on 12 words of their own at the end.

To further their Conservative subterfuge Scalia's Court claimed that because the District of Columbia was technically not a state, it's gun laws were unconstitutional.

I believe it was John Dean, America's unforgiven patriot, who observed that Conservatives view the Constitution of the United States, not as a Rule of Law, nor as a playbook, but rather a blob of Play Dough to be molded in service of Conservative doxology – Scalia's ruling in *Heller* being an alarming example of just such an assault on the Bill of Rights."

"In *Citizens United v. Federal Election Commission,* (2010) Conservative extremist Supreme Court Judge Scalia, unconstitutionally appointed by Conservative extremist Reagan, ruled that the extremist Conservative organization  Citizens United,, as a corporation was a *de facto* association of individuals, who as individuals would enjoy 'unrestricted expenditures for political communication under the First Amendment right of free speech, which as a corporation made up of individuals, have that same right. (That's the same compartmentalized logic which permits Scalia's Catholic Church to vote a human Pope – the now suddenly more than  human "Holy Father" to be worshiped as a transient God. )

It has long been concluded that Republicans are the party of  money and Democrats the party of numbers – Republicans win by outspending the Democrats, Democrats win by having more voters.

It's a class war, of course, so, as night follows day, Democrats try, with little success, to limit the amount of money campaigns can raise, while Republicans,with more money and therefore more success, try to limit the number of voters,

The most notorious example being Katherine Harris, Florida's Secretary of State, Supervisor of Elections and simultaneously, co-chair of Bush II's 2000 Florida presidential Campaign! (Only in Florida would such a flagrant and illegal conflict of interest prevail! It can be said that Florida is to the United States what Australia was to England – a place for crooks and criminals). So Katherine Harris, Florida's Secretary of State, Supervisor of Elections and simultaneously, co-chair of Bush II's 2000 Florida presidential Campaign, (1) Illegally purged thousands of minority (Democrat) felons from the voter rolls, (2) Halted the vote recount to favor Bush over Gore, (2) Certified the election results after halting the recount to favor Bush over Gore, (3) Had her Certification voided by the Florida Supreme Court, only to be approved  by the unconstitutional Scalia ("my court" ) US Supreme Court, in *Bush v.Gore. "*-- Conservative 'dirty tricks', to wit, Scalia's US Supreme Court, remanded back to Florida Supreme Court, knowing the safe harbor deadline had passed, meaning procedure trumped justice - - Harris's bogus recount giving Florida to Bush by 537 votes, the 25 Electoral College votes, and therefore, the Presidency of the United States – the presidency of the United States determined by two conspiring Conservative crooks – Scalia and Harris."

Brody: "Your Honor, I again object most strongly to the Defendant's rambling, irrelevant, conclusory, discourse as to the late exemplary Justice Scalia."

Judge Vance: I concur. Move on."

Dr. Otis: "The Prosecutor challenged me to defend my 'Must Remove Book," which is that Trump, having made fraudulent promises to the voter to induce them to vote for him, which he knew or should have known, were not his constitutionally to make, that voters did vote for him, and that voters were injured – damaged – pandemic deaths and lost jobs and homes, as a result of Trump's presidency, thereby meeting the test of fraud. An instance of Fraud vitiates the most solemn contracts, documents, and judgments, *US v. Throckmorton.*  Trump, described his presidency as his 'Contract with America,' therefore, his fraudulent acts, vitiate that contract, in turn voiding Trump's presidency."

Brody: "You're not serious."

Dr. Otis: "Serious that 'no man is above the law' is the cornerstone of America's judicial system, serous that 'all men are created equal,' serious that Trump named his presidency "My contract with America,' and serious that fraud vitiates everything – contracts. pursuant to *US v. Throckmorton*? I could not be more serious! Trump's  presidency is null and void, as a matter of law."

Brody: "I get it. You're claiming an insanity defense."

Dr. Otis: "This Court is denying me my 14th Amendment rights to equal protections under the laws by allowing sarcasm by the goose, but not the gander."

Judge Vance; "Over-ruled."

Brody; "And this has to do with his Honorable Supreme Court Judge Scalia, how, I should be afraid to ask?"

Dr. Otis: "Just as Scalia had re-written the Second Amendment in *Heller,* extreme ConservativeScalia, in *Citizens United,* rewrote the First Amendment to make the preposterous, unconscionable, incompetent self-serving fantasy claim the corporations are individuals, and as individuals, have a First Amendment right to free speech, to make unlimited, unrestricted, independent expenditures for political communication, a ruling right out of Scalia's catholic compartmentalized mind incapable of seeing that *Citizens United,* bought and paid for extreme Conservative governance of the United States for many generation, in effect plunging the final and fatal dagger into the heart of the Constitutional Republic."

Brody: "According to you – an eighty-four year-old – over the hill by 25 years -- defrocked psychologist, with no credential in law, or political science."

Dr. Otis: "Truth, alone is the final arbiter of all claims to knowledge."

Brody: "The only irrefutable truth in these matters is that you , and you alone, not only assassinated  Donald J. Trump. President of the United States, but you had been planning to do it since he was inaugurated. Your Honor, Peoples 5-20 -- a sample of the Defendant's tweets from 2015 to the present claimed to have been drafted by the Defendant in his brand name "Uncommon Sense." Please read People's # One."

Dr. Otis: "-- I say having tried Special Prosecutor Mueller, who blinked, and impeachment. which treasonous Republican Senators sabotaged by voting Conservative Republican Party over duty to Country, we "bury" Trump if that presumes a body to bury."

Brody: "Sounds like a plot to assassinate President Trump to me."

Dr. Otis: "In the ear of the listener. The word 'we' bars you  from such a conclusion."

Brody: "Please read tweet number two.."

Dr. Otis: "--Trump, Hannity, Carlson, Limbaugh, Trump's political/ whore/press secretary McEnany, AG Barr, Mitch McConnell, pompous ass Pompeo. Senator 'Lily' Graham, FOX  Propagandists -- Liars everyone who should be taken out and shot for treason – crimes against the United States."

Brody: "Mass murderer, too. Tweet number three."

Dr. Otis: "--Trump's unconscionable, corrupt, pardon of convicted Stone, just another day in the depraved presidency of Donald Trump who, before the Conservative 50-year coup of the Constitutional Republic became a *fait accompli* in 2016, would have died a Mussolini death on the streets of DC."

Brody: "Tweet number four."

Dr. Otis   " --Suppose someone had assassinated Hitler to save Germany from itself … Hero? Patriot? Assassin?"

Brody: "Assassin. I have no further questions of the Defendant, but reserve the right to recall him at some future time.

Judge Vance: "Court is adjourned  until

tomorrow morning at 10."


# Day Four


Brody; "The Prosecution calls Dr. Golden to the Stand. .... "Your name?"

"Sam Golden, MD."

Brody: "You are a Psychiatrist licensed by the American Psychiatric Association and professor Emeritus from Georgetown":

Dr. Golden. "I am both."

Brody: "And a law degree?"

Dr. Golden: "I do. Also Georgetown. Undergraduate at Johns Hopkins."

Brody: "Did you perform a court-ordered psychiatric examination of the Defendant Richard Otis,"

Dr. Golden: "I did."

Brody: "Did the Defendant cooperate?"

Dr. Golden; "It was awkward for both of us, but I would say ,"yes." Court-ordered evaluations by their very nature, present special restraints, challenges, and contaminants.."

Brody: "Are you satisfied that your findings are an accurate representation of the Defendant's psychiatric status at the time of the alleged assassination of President Trump?"

Dr. Golden; "I am."

Brody: "Would you mind  telling the Court what strategies, tasks or tests you administered to reach your findings?"

Dr. Golden: "Standard Psychiatric Evaluation – neurological screening for gross motor dysfunction, background including medical, drug, law enforcement, education, and family history and clinical interview."

Brody; "Leaving no stones unturned."

Dr. Golden: "That's the  plan."

Brody: "And your clinical findings summarized for the Court?"

Dr. Golden: "Neurologically the client was --"

Brody; "-- The Defendant Richard Otis --"

Dr. Golden: "--was asymptomatic -- Seemed to show no signs of gross neurological impairment such as would be revealed in abnormal reflexes, articulation problems, loss of balance, memory loss, motor control – walking problems, which, in turn, could be symptoms of a seizure disorder, Parkinson's Disease, stroke, dementia, multiple sclerosis,  and traumatic brain disorder."

Brody; "You found no evidence of neurological impairment which could be the direct cause of the charges against the Defendant"

Dr. Golden: "Correct. Dr. Otis did complain of frequent loss of balance, memory loss, gait problems – losing control of his legs after walking for distances of a quarter of a mile and longer and wondered – worried – that his father's history of multiple sclerosis, his sister's history of Parkinson's, and his loss of control of his legs might represent a continuum of a common genetic disorder. I explained I knew of no such hypothesis. I also explained that I have no expertise in psychiatric gerontology and was therefore unable to separate his neurological complaints from those predicted to be normal in an 84 year-old male. Dr.

Otis's only hospitalizations wee for a tonsillectomy at age 10, and double hip replacements at age 71, due to osteoarthritis. Dr. Otis claims he has never smoked a single cigarette nor had a can of beer, arguing that at 5/9 and weighing 160 pounds inhigh school – his current weight 66 years later, and wanting to play left field for the Boston Red Sox, he could ill afford the ills of smoking or drinking, so he never did eitherone. Dr. Otis states he has exercised regularly all his life, and currently jogs, works out with dumbbells, and does 75 push-ups every day except cutting back when the heat is over 97, typically eliminating one of the three exercises. He reports having lifted weights competitively, once  bench – pressing 400 pounds for six repetitions , and another time dead-lifting 600 pounds – both times weighing 160-165. (He says about a year or two ago, he was stopped by a Virginia Highway patrolman, who upon noting Dr. Otis's  date of birth on his driver's license. age threatened to arrest Dr. Otis, for altering his  driver's license. I admit to being suspicious myself until I realized only teenagers add years to the date of birth on their ID. Dr. Otis, denies a history of illicit  and licit drug use or abuse, even noting he doesn't even stock aspirin or pain medicine cabinet, once in the 70's having written the hardback, *Is Your Prescription  Killing You?* The exception being Tums for chronic reflux disease.

As to his schooling, he admits hating his father for having deceived him into going for a Labor Day visit to his father, his new step-mother, his 6.month-old half-brother, and his younger sister and brother who, had gone to a separate foster home, and out of sight for the past six years, and when he, his adoptive

grandmother and grandfather got ready to leave, he was
told by his grandmother – not his father, -- that he
wasn't going home, but was staying with this father.

Dr. Otis contends the schools were so bad, that
when he managed to get his father mad enough to get
thrown out and sent back to his grandmother, he had to
repeat most of his  classes and so far behind he never
did catch up until  his sophomore year in college. He
received no financial help so it took him 6 years to get
his BA, during which he attended four different
colleges. His father had graduated from high school, his
mother had dropped out, and none of his siblings or half
siblings had earned a college degree'

Dr. Otis's family history would have predicted
far more psychopathology than appears to be the case.
His mother, who was raised believing her mother was
her much older sister, and her father was her brother-in-
law in order to "reframe" the adultery of her parents,
reportedly abandoned Dr. Otis at the front door of a
Boston foster home when he was four, never to be seen
or heard from again. (She was living in Yakima,
Washington when she died of a blood clot at age 32.
His father, adopted from an orphanage at age two,
may never have bonded with his adoptive father, who
was fighting Germans in the trenches of France
in World War I, during the "bonding period,": and who
never measured up to the rigors of his Puritanical
adoptive mother, who never forgave him for his
compulsion  to find his biological mother.

The Great Depression, divorce, disappointing
his adoptive father as being physically unfit to military
service, a factory injury causing him to lose three
fingers, and incurring multiple sclerosis at age 35,

appears to have so psychologically wounded his father that he could not be the father young Richard  needed and desired. Absent a mother and father to trust and take care of him and surrounded by adults who were not his biological relatives, teenage Richard, unable to trust anyone to love, protect, and parent him, he was forced to raise himself --"

Brody; "Go it alone.'

Dr. Golden: "Do that which others could not, or would not, do for him."

Brody; "--"Take matters into his own hands."

Dr. Golden; "Because he believed he has to "

Brody: "Assassinate the President of the United States --"

Dr. Golden: " – Not because he wanted to, but because no one else would."

Brody; " The Prosecution rests."

Judge Vance: "Does the Defendant have any questions of this witness?"

Dr. Otis: "Dr. Golden, Hypothetically,  could a person convinced by the evidence  over the past three years, shared by 63% of  Americans, that the President of the United States, represents clear and present danger to the Republic, acknowledge all other options have been tried and failed, consider getting rid of said enemy, without necessarily presuming psychopathology as defined in DSM-5?

Dr. Golden: "Hypothetically?

Dr. Otis: "Hypothetically"

Dr. Golden. "Yes, I suppose so."

Dr. Otis; "No further questions

Judge Vance."The Defense may present its case.

Dr. Otis: "Jurors, I see in your faces the same fear, anxiety, and doubt I too have felt since 2015, beginning with these questions, (1) Are the Republicans really going to nominate someone with no experience and no training, known to me only as someone on TV who got off telling his employees, "You're fired," itself causing me to ask, what kind of person enjoys publicly humiliating his employees, by firing them? (2) Did the person running as the Republican presidential candidate just slander his Democratic opponent Hillary Clinton as "Killer Hillary", inciting those at his rally to chant "Lock her up, Lock her up," knowing Hillary Clinton was never charged or convicted of causing the death of anyone? (3) My neighbor in Elizabeth City, North Carolina slandered President Obama, claiming Obama was born in Kenya, not an US citizen , and therefore an illegal president, who also forged his transcript to get into Harvard, and also cheated on tests to keep from flunking out. When I asked for the source of the information, my neighbor cited an interview Trump had with Sean Hannity on Fox News. (4) Avoiding FOX for the Conservative propaganda fraud that it is, I asked, had Trump ever made such criminally liable, fraudulent, depraved statements, and if he had, how could he still be allowed to run for the presidency? (5) Trump promises he will build a wall to keep Mexican immigrants from seeking the better life as advertised by United States and to force the President of Mexico to pay for it. Didn't Trump know that Congress, not the President of the United States, funds and orders interstate/international walls to be built, and that Trump cannot order any foreign government to do anything? If he didn't know, what is he doing running for President?

Less than 24 hours after Trump's  inauguration, Trump proved he was mentally disqualified from being the President by creating his own realty, to wit that his inaugural audience was "thousands more than President Obama's inaugural audience." "We had the biggest audience in the history of inaugural speeches," and, "This was the greatest audience to ever witness a inauguration – period --both in person and around the globe," (Spicer), when photos of both inaugural audiences showed Obama's wall to wall – Washington Monument to Capitol – a vast sea of people shoulder to shoulder, while photos of the same area during Trump's inauguration revealed large vast empty spaces of grass. (Narcissistic Personality Disorder – Symptom #1- "grandiose sense of self importance—exaggerates achievements"

One week after being sworn in,Trump committed the crime of obstruction of justice when he made an implied threat to FBI Director James Comey to either disappear the FBI's investigation of Russia's influence in electing Trump and defeating Hillary Clinton, or be fired.

Trump fired Comey, and in so doing to effect the outcome of a pending investigation, Trump committed the crime of obstruction of justice.

Why wasn't Trump tried, found guilty of the crime of obstruction of justice, jailed and removed from office? Because Conservative Republican controlled US Dept. of Justice in the person of Special Prosecutor Robert Mueller, stated, "Department of Justice agency policy" – not rules, not statute, mot law forbade convicting a sitting president," that's why.

Discovering, that which he already knew, to wit, that Trump alone was above the law, throughout the four years of his presidency his crimes against the United States and the American citizenry would continue in severity and frequency.

No one seemed to realize, or if they did, said or did nothing, that the Coney incident demonstrated a fatal flaw in Trump's governance – he had been elected, albeit by a minority of voters, President, but believed, behaved, and spoke as if he were a banana republic's ruthless, take-no-prisoners, self-serving,narcissistic dictator – who was not only above the law, but maker of the law, and breaker of the law.

For example, a month into his presidency, Trump appointed sycophant, Napoleonic, arch-southern racist, extreme Republican Conservative, Jeff Sessions as his Attorney General. (Sessions  had lied during his Senate confirmation vetting that he had had no contacts with the Russians.) In fact, Trump appointed Sessions Attorney General expecting – insisting -- Sessions sabotage the FBI's probe into the Russian meddling in the US election to help elect Trump, thereby committing a second  obstruction of justice crime.)

So when Sessions recused himself from the Russian investigation, Trump went ballistic, launching personal attacks on Sessions  – "Jeff Sessions is very weak – DISGRACEFUL," and  finally firing Sessions on November 7, 2018.

Trump commits another criminal act of obstruction of justice by allegedly assuring his former

Presidential Campaign Manager Paul Manafort a pardon if he "takes one" for Trump.

In an even more egregious example of criminal obstruction of justice, Trump pardoned his close friend and :partner in earlier crimes, Roger Stone, whose original sentence recommendation by the Justice Department for Stone's seven felony convictions had been 7-9 years, already reduced by Attorney Barr to 40 months –obstruction of justice, causing the original prosecuting attorneys to resign.

Trump criminally conspired with McConnell and Senate Conservative Republicans, to violate the Constitution's  guarantee of a fair and impartial judiciary for all citizens., by (1) Refusing to do as the Constitution required -- vote on President's Obama's Supreme Court nominee Merrick Garland, (2)  Waiting until Republican Conservative Trump was in office to appoint Republican Conservative Gorsuch to the Supreme Court, (3) Appointing as many federal Conservative Republican judges as Trump could identify, for the sole illicit and unconstitutional purpose of perpetuating a Conservative Republican biased federal judiciary incapable of providing a fair and impartial judiciary  for generations, and (4) Rushing to appoint another Conservative Republican Supreme Court Judge,  Kavanaugh before ascertaining that judge, as a college student who bragged he "loved beer,"  had raped a female classmate.

Next, Trump, on tape, committed the crimes bribery, extortion, unlawfully involving a foreign country in the internal affairs of the United States, unlawfully involving a foreign country in the election of the US President, stating Trump would release military aid to  Ukraine, which had already been allocated by Congress, and therefore not Trump's to withhold, contingent on Ukraine 's government getting "dirt" on Democratic candidate Joe Biden and his son, as to their relationships with the Ukraine government and a private company.

A whistleblower was the first to report the incident, which was subsequently corroborated by the testimony of career diplomats and state department staff, during the House of  Representative's Impeachment hearing.

Trump first lied – perjured himself -- that such communication between himself and the President of Ukraine  ever happened, next denied a *quid pro qua* ever existed, and then demanded the name of the whistleblower, which was, of course, not allowed by Whistleblower Law.

Trump was impeached, but just as the Conservative Republican Justice Department aided and abetted Trump's escape from prison by citing bogus policy – not law – that a sitting president was above the law, this time Trump was handed  a "Get Out of Jail Free' pass by the totally corrupt treasonous Conservative Republican Senators, who voted Party over Country.

.It was apparent to me that the Conservative takeover of America begun in 1954, when, by Executive Order, Eisenhower decreed that the Pledge of Allegiance be amended by inserting the words "under God," thereby voiding the sacrosanct doctrine of separation of church and state, thus opening the doors of Congress to religion zealots, particularly the false prophets for profit from the south like millionaire Billy

Graham, had 60 years later become a *fait accompli* during the reign of Dictator Donald "The Terrible" Trump.

Just as Hitler gained control of the government, the courts, the military, business, and the message – propaganda --"I am der Fuhrer -- The Jew is the enemy."

Trump gained control of the government by appointments of agency directors,the US Supreme Court and Federal Courtsby nominating only Conservative judges, the military as Commander in Chief, (Trump's dad paid a New York podiatrist to find a bone spur so his Donnie could avoid serving his country in the Vietnam War), Big Business – Trump was their Poster Boy, or their Frankenstein's Monster, depending on how much your bank would loan you, and the message – FOX NEWs – FOX CONSERVATIVE PROPAGANDA,"I am the greatest President ever --The immigrant is the enemy."

Trump's coup of America was different that Hitler's coup of Germany only as to Hitler's military excesses and better oratory.

In 2018,, Trump disbanded President Obama's 2014 White House National; Security Council Directorate for Global Health, Security and Biodefense created to establish federal coordination against pandemics, arguing, "I'm a ----businessman, so I don't like having thousands of people I don't need."

December 2019, China's Huber province reports 802 cases of coronavirus.

January 21, 2020, the first case of coronavirus is reported in the United States.

January 22, 2020. Trump is asked if he is worried about the coronavirus, to which Trump answers, "No not at all. We have it totally under control."

February, 24, 2020. Trump: "The Coronavirus is very much under control in the USA The stock market is starting to look very good to me."

March 6, 2020. Trump: "And in terms of deaths, I don't know the count is today. Is it eleven And in terms of cases it's very very few… Anybody that needs a test can have a test They are all set ."

April 17, 2020 Trump, out of one side of his mouth put the COVID –19 pandemic on the state governors to do the testing, provide the masks, protective garments, the hospital beds and doctors – in effect "own" the virus. Out of the other side of his mouth, Trump exploitsCOVID-19 to his political advantage by

propagandizing that states with Democratic governors, whose protesters – defiant Trump supporters claiming it's a  "free country" – the government has no right to make me wear a mask and no right to make me stay at home instead of going to my favorite bar, should  open NOW.

So  on April 17, 2020, Trump, demonstrating once again, his criminally depraved indifference to human life – his treacherous sacrifice of the death of Americans to win an election, tweets "Liberate Michigan", "Liberate Minnesota,"  and  to Virginia, :"Save our great 2$^{nd}$ Amendment!"

By April 30, 2020, 56,225 Americans had died from COVID -19,

On April 22, Trump suspends payments to the World Health Organization.

By May 30th, 102,796, Americans had died from COVID-19

June 30, 126,615, Americans had died from COVID-19.

July 30, 150,908, Americans had died from COVID-19

Meanwhile, Trump played golf every weekend, he still had not provided a coordinated federal plan as other countries had done, testing was state to state – haphazard -- law of the jungle affair with states competing with other states for testing materials, masks, safety and protective gear, ventilators, and Trump's claim on March 6, that anybody who needs a teat can have a test was as much a lie on August 6, 2020, as it had been on March 6, 2020.

Trump, unable to provide competent leadership or initiative publically offers Americans  two fatal cures – ingest disinfectants,  which is, on its face is both deplorable, and laughable, until realizing: (1) Trumpists, loyal out of ignorance, might take Trump's advice, and (2)Trump is so deluded with his intellectual prowess that he actually believed he had come up with an ingenious scientifically workable cure, that had escaped the world's health experts.

Trump's second proffered cure for COVID -19 is a drug called Hydroxychloroquine which, despite medical evidence it is not only ineffective in the treatment of COVID –19, but can be fatal by causing heart arrhythmia, was just days ago, reinvented as a cure by a bogus Trump tweet, which was immediately pulled off Twitter and Facebook as a hoax.

The questions which must now be asked are these. (1) What percentage of Americans who died from COVID-!9 died as the direct result of Trump's first 60 days of denying  the coronavirus threatened Americans? (2) What percentage of Americans who died from COVID-!9 died as the direct result of Trump's sabotaging of America's testing effort ?(3) What percentage of Americans who died from COVID-!9 died as the direct result of Trump's gross negligence in providing Federal assistance in testing, obtaining masks, ventilators,  and protective gear for first responders, nurses, and doctors? (4) What percentage of Americans who died from COVID-!9 died as the direct result of Trump sabotaging efforts of the medical experts to close non-essential business and businesses where large numbers of people would be in close contact with other people? (5) What percentage of Americans who died from COVID-!9 died as the direct result of Trump's pressuring states to open before the case numbers justified opening and without a plan for opening? (6) What percentage of Americans who died from COVID-!9 died as the direct result of Trump sacrificing American lives on the altar of his reelection?

On May 25, 2020 American's watched the night's news in horror as Minneapolis police officer Derek Chauvin nonchalantly kneeled on a downed George Floyd's neck for nine minutes, during which Mr. Floyd pleaded, "I can't breathe!" until a medic arrived and told Chauvin Mr. Floyd was dead.

Evidence of Chauvin's execution of Mr. Floyd was gleaned from the fact Chauvin's hand remained in his pocket the entire nine minutes as if Chauvin was simply waiting for Mr. Floyd to die, and the fact that Chauvin's  fellow officers acted as lookouts.

What was Mr. Floyd's life worth? According to the Minneapolis police, $20.00 -- the amount Mr. Floyd was suspected of cashing as an alleged counterfeit $20 dollar bill

As predicted, Trump's initial response to Mr. Floyd's murder by police Officer Cauvin was formal, sanitized, insincere, prepared, and read – a pause before Trump's inevitable storm of racism, hate, and exploitation from the real Donald Trump, who promptly switched from the murder of a black man by a white cop to deriding protesters as "thugs," when "looting begins, shooting starts," to calling protesters "terrorists", "arsonists," "criminals," and "anarchists," threatening to use Federal troops in "these cities run by liberal Democrats," to illegally sending Federal troops into to Portland, Oregon, after being told not to by the Oregon Governor and the mayor of Portland, unwittingly  stomping on the Republican's sacred cow - -"States Rights", since the 1850's

It was all another Trumpian ruse – "dirty trick" by a panicked Trump, who frantically grasping at straws, drew "tricky Dick" Nixon's "law and order" straw.

Suddenly, lawless above the law Trump had changed his spots.

In the beginning, it seemed to work -- His federal military invasion of Portland, Oregon increased the violence, which Trump then claimed, proved his need to send in his troops.

Not exactly, because when his troops left, the violence decreased.

`        Perhaps the most Hitleresque moment in Trump's depraved presidency occurred on June 1, 2020, when US Attorney General Barr, with no jurisdiction in the city of Washington, DC, suddenly ordered the military-style police to forcibly remove all George Floyd peaceful protesters exercising their First Amendment right to peacefully assemble and to free speech, from Lafayette Square.

        Police, some on horses, charged the peaceful protesters, striking them withshields as night sticks and battering rams, spraying the unarmed protesterswith pepper spray, shooting them with rubber bullets, firing tear gas canisters at them, and intimidating them with low flying helicopters, until the protesters had been cleared from Lafayette Square.

        The cause for Attorney General Barr's Gestapo tactics?

        Minutes earlierin a Rose Garden speech, Trump, who had just anointed himself the "law and order President," demanded Barr clear the road from the Rose Garden to St. John's Church, of all protesters, so His Most Unholy of Holinesses could paradeto the Church, where, holding a Bible, as if for the first time, Trump sanctified his new title as "law and order President" celebrated with a photo-op.

        In another example of Trump's rampant and treacherous politicizing of Federal agencies to gain Hitleresque control of the Government, Trump's mega-donor Louis DeJoy, who donated $2.1 million, to Trump's Victory Fund and millions more to the Republican Party, on May 6, 2020, became Postmaster General.

His first order of business was to change the US Postal Service into US Postal Offices, Inc. and under the ruse of a business model, instead of a service model, established policies – leaving arriving mail on the floor at 5 o'clock, eliminating overtime, and late deliveries, just in time to aid and abet Trump's criminal enterprise of destroying the public's trust in the Postal Service, in turn, sabotaging mail-in ballots to burden Democrat voters, thereby fraudulently and criminally rigging the 2020 election .

Trump's was fraudulently elected in 2016, with the help of Putin. He's counting on being elected in 2020, now aided and abetted by his  just appointed, bought and paid for, Postmaster General DeJoy – nepotism, fraud, voter suppression, and obstruction of justice.

John Lewis civil rights icon, 'Brother" of Rev. Martin Luther King, who organized the March on Washington, son of Alabama sharecropper, US Congress House of Representatives since 1986, and awarded Medal of Freedom by President Obama, died on July 17, putting the Country in morning for the next two weeks.

Three former presidents spoke at his funeral and a forth, 95 year-old Jimmy Carter, sent a letter, which was read by the pastor. President Obama's eulogy received a standing ovation.

And why was Trump notably absent? Two reasons. Trump never plays second fiddle, even if first fiddle is dead. Second, Trump holds grudges, and is without, mercy, empathy, and forgiveness, and once attacked Mr. Lewis as , "All talk, talk, talk, talk -- no action or results. Sad."

Trump is wrong 99% of the time.

Loved and admired "Little Giant" US Supreme Court Justice Ruth Bader Ginsburg dies. While her diminutive body is still warm, Trump exploits her death by announcing he will immediately nominate a Conservative judge to replace her before the election43 days hence!.

The Constitution of the United States guarantees all  citizens a  "fair and impartial Federal judiciary.

By nominating Judge Barrett, a known Conservative extremist and Scalia wannabe, Trump not only violates his oath as President to 'protect and defend the Constitution, but exploits Conservative extremist nominee Judge Barrett as a personal vendetta to defeat  former President Obama's Affordable Care Act, as Trump had promised he would do to get elected.

Furthermore, by nominating a young Judge Barrett, as  he had done with "I- love-beer' Kavanaugh, Trump again denies Americans a "fair and  impartial federal judiciary' for decades --  a wanton  abuse of power,  inviting the criminal charge of  obstruction of justice..

As  a result of two political parties in the Rose Garden, one celebrating the nomination of Judge Barrett, in which, few wore masks, and  "social distancing" was also ignored,  19 attendees, including Trump, tested  positive for Covid-19, as the direct result of Trump's refusal to play by the rules.

As soon as Trump was released,.  He began a frantic, last minute  series of rallies – all against  the state's policy  of wearing  masks and maintaining social distancing  -- Trump one again   putting his supporters at risk on the altar of his re-election. Some will die? Statistically, yes.

So it iss that in less than  four years, Trump overthrew the Constitutional Republic in favor of a Putin-like  dictatorship with Trump installed for life.

The blame for Trump's presidency, aka "Four Year's Tenancy in Satan's House," is better placed at the doorstep of the Republican National Committee than on  Trump's, threshold, as Trump could rightfully plead not guilty by reason of insanity.

Trump's diagnosis of Narcissistic Personality Disorder, is noted for its delusions – craziness – insanity, whereas a cursory vetting by the Republican National Committee would have warned them Trump is crazy, unstable, not a team player, and a clear and present danger to remake the Republican Party in his delusional image of himself.

Blame also needs to visit the American Psychiatric Association and the American Psychological Association which both had a duty to inform Congress that Trump must be disqualified as a presidential candidate, or must be disqualified pursuant to Amendment 25 of the Constitution, given his diagnosis of a severe untreatable mental disorder, which was both predictable and avoidable, to wit, his every behavior demonstrated one or more of the nine symptoms of a Narcissistic Personality Disorder,

For my part, I expected the Republicans to nix Trump's candidacy for the reasons just cited, my fellow psychiatrist and psychologists to do their duty to their professions and Country by disqualifying Trump due to his mental disorder, Special Prosecutor Robert Mueller to rule on the evidence, not according to the contrived

corrupt policy of Trump's Department of Justice  that Trump was above the law, that Conservative Republican Senators would vote Country  and conscience to Impeach Trump as the evidence and testimony demanded, instead of committing
treason by voting Conservative Republican Party over duty to Country, that Americans would take to the streets demanding Trump resign due to the thousands of deaths caused by Trump sacrificing American lives so he could get elected.

No one did, so I -- a most reluctant patriot put my duty to my Country over my own life."
Judge Vance; "Is the Prosecution able to make its Closing Statement at this time?"

Brody: "We can your Honor if we might be granted a short recess."

Judge Vance: "The Defense?"

Dr. Otis: "The Defense has no objection"

Judge Vance. "This Court stands adjourned until 2pm."


## Day Four --Afternoon


Judge Vance: "Is the Prosecution ready to make its Closing Statement?"

Brody; "The Prosecution is Ready, Your Honor."

Judge Vance: "You may proceed."

Brody: "Members of the jury, speaking on behalf of this Court, District Attorney Barr, the Department of Justice, my staff, and the citizens of the United States, I personally  thank you for performing this thankless task of civic jury duty, without which there would be no courts, no system of justice, and no democracy. Again, on behalf of all your fellow American citizens, I thank you.

That said, the Defendant has unintentionally made your task a slam dunk due to the fact that the Defendant admits he assassinated Donald J. Trump, President of the United States, we have eye-witnesses who saw the drone fire the shot that killed the President as he exited his helicopter,  the Defendant admitted  he purchased, re-configured, and operated the drone used to assassinate President Trump, the Defendant's fingerprints were taken from the downed drone --Like I said, a slam dunk.

So why has the Government of the United States incurred all this time and expense and caused you to be taken away from your family and friends?

Because the Defendant wants to quibble over the meaning of the word "assassinate' like Clinton wanted to knit-pick over the word "sex"

Faced with the reality of a lethal injection, the Defendant now wants us to make an exception for him by changing "assassination" to defense of Country' as if he were a soldier in uniform in Afghanistan.

I know it's easy to forget, with all the tedious and trifling cognitive dissonant ramblings from the Defendant, but the Judge did remind you that Title18 U.S. Code #1111, defines "murder" as the unlawful killing of a human being with malice of aforethought – premeditated –planned in advance – is murder in the first degree to be punished by death or by imprisonment for life. 18 U.S. Code IIII specifically lists causing the death of the President of the United States a capital offense for which the death sentence must be imposed.

So there you have it – a slam dunk! For murdering – assassinating President Trump,, the Defendant must be put to death by lethal injection.

Not exactly.The Defendant, at first deluded, like Lee Harvey Oswald, that assassinating the President would make him an instant hero, now faced with the reality the State is instead going to kill him – what goes round comes around, would have you believe that he acted in defense of the United States –

I know from the looks on your faces that you find the Defendant's argument incredible. I agree,. but in our system of justice, the accused is presumed innocent until  proven  guilty in a court of law by a jury of his peers and that everyone has a First Amendment right to his or her day in court.

So we come together today at this time in history and at this place, to render a judgment as to the Defendant's guilt or innocence as to the charge, under Title 18 U.S.C. 1751 Section # 1111 – First Degree Murder of the President of the United States, one Donald J. Trump.

I have here in my hand two books written by the Defendant – One titled "Why And How We The People Must Remove Trump." – remove meaning get rid of – assassinate, where you will read –  see for yourselves, in the Defendants own words, his stated reasons for assassinating President Trump, and his second book, "Trump's Troops Revolt Against Republican Party's Betrayal," – the Prosecution's double-barrel smoking gun – the Defendant's written admission of his guilt.

If it seems to you as it does to me, that the Defendant suddenly awoke to the reality that the Government of the United States, with your help, is going to put the needle of death in his arm unless he could concoct the cockamamie, story that because President Trump had become such an enemy of the people and of the United States, and because all legal attempts to remove Trump  had failed – failed because there was no basis for alleging the President had committed any crimes.

The Defendant's chutzpah defense out of the way, and his guilt established, let us consider motive, and for that, we look to others who have also assassinated the President of the United  States.

On April 14, 1865,John Wilkes Booth, made his way into the Ford Theater where President Lincoln was in attendance, sneaked up behind Lincoln and shot him in the head. Lincoln died the next morning.

Booth hiding  in a barn, which was torched by Union forces, was killed as he fled the fire.

The other members of the conspiracy were hanged.

On July 2, 1881,Charles Guiteau, having had his application for Ambassador of France personally rejected by President Garfield, shot  Garfield at short range, and was hung for his crime.

September 6,1901, Leon Czolgosz,  shot President McKinley twice in the stomach as McKinley was greeting the public at the Pan-American Exposition in Buffalo, NY

Czolgosz was electrocuted.

Democrat President John F. Kennedy was ambushed and killed by Lee Harvey Oswald on Friday

November 22, 1963 at 12:30 P.M,  as Kennedy was riding in an open car in a presidential motorcade as it passed through Dealey Plaza in Dallas, Texas

Oswald was subsequently killed by Jack Ruby as Oswald was in police custody, thereby leaving the world to speculate as to why Oswald killed Kennedy.

Dr. Diamond, psychologist, reasoned Oswald, whose father died before Oswald was born, made Oswald feel less a man, with a compulsion to do something real big on the world's stage. – what bigger thing to do than to assassinate the President of the United State, John Kennedy?

The Defendant, who admittedly hated his weak "loser" father, made the Defendant feel less a man, with a compulsion to do something real big on the world's stage.– what bigger thing to do than to assassinate the President of the United States, Donald Trump?

Case precedent is clear and inexorable: You kill the president of the United States, for whatever reason or motive, and you die at the hands of the State.

As to the case at bar, the Defendant's claim that President Trump was a threat to the Republic and its citizens is at odds with the data that shows the President enjoys 91% approval ratings among Republicans

The Defendant cannot simultaneously argue that President Trump was such a threat to the United States and its citizens to warrant assassination whileacknowledging a 91% approval rating among 40% of the population.

18 U.S. Code IIII specifically lists causing the death of the President of the United States to be a capital offense for which the death sentence must be imposed.

We need to proceed no further. Pursuant to Title 18 U.S. Code 175 Section 1111  the jury must find the Defendant guilty of causing the death of the President of the United States, Donald Trump, and must be put to death.

Thank you."

Judge Vance: "The Defendant may proceed with his closing statement.

Dr. Otis; Mr.Brody falsely characterizes my action as unlawful killing with malice aforethought, when the State knows, or should know, from the set of facts presented, that rather than 'malice  aforethought,' I acted out fear that the beloved Country of my childhood was becoming a Country of shame, lead by Hitleresque propagandist Donald J. Trump, who put self *uber alles*, and who, like the HitlerI had known second-hand as a young boy, was a ruthless bully – a control freak – consensus enemy of the people and the State!

When all political entities failed – failed by the very reason of Trump's absolute control of those political entities, just as any soldier would act militarily to defend America, I acted in my civic duty to defend America against a known Hitleresque dictator in the act of overthrowing the Government of the United States for a Putin-like Oligarchy with Trump becoming Putin-West.

Therefore, having failed to prove 'malice aforethought' as required by Title18 U.S.C. section1751, #llll, Mr. Brody's case must be dismissed as a matter of law.

Pursuant to Federal Rules of Civil Procedure Rule 29,(a) the Defendant herein submits a Motion for a

Judgment of Acquittal before the case is submitted to the jury.

This Court, on the Defendant's motion must enter a judgment of acquittal of any offense for which evidence is insufficient to sustain a conviction."

Judge Vance. "The Court reserves its decision."

,_______________________________________

—

*Washington News*

# OTIS BEHEADED BY TRUMP GANG!

WASHINGTON,DC – A gang of white males brandishing automatic weapons, wearing Trump shirts, red hats & black ski masks, jumped from their black cargo truck after rammingthe police van returning Dr. Otis to jail pending a jury verdict,disarmed thepolice guards, who made little or no resistance, beheaded Otis, tossed his head into their truck, and were last seen heading  toward 395 South, reportedly under informal DC police escort.